BLOOD IN PARADISE

When a new railroad threatens the peace of the beautiful, unspoilt Paradise Valley, a chain of senseless killings explodes, and Tom Blood, railroad detective and gunfighter, is sent for. Experienced though Blood is, this mission tests his every skill as he faces corruption, intrigue and brutal murder. Only his grim determination to win against all odds can bring peace and justice to a troubled land.

Books by R. M. Litchfield
in the Linford Western Library:

BLOOD WILL HAVE BLOOD

R. M. LITCHFIELD

BLOOD IN PARADISE

Complete and Unabridged

LINFORD
Leicester

First published in Great Britain in 1995 by
Robert Hale Limited
London

First Linford Edition
published 2001
by arrangement with
Robert Hale Limited
London

British Library CIP Data

Litchfield, R. M.
    Blood in Paradise.—Large print ed.—
Linford western library
    1. Western stories
    2. Large type books
    I. Title
    823.9'14 [F]

    ISBN 0-7089-5921-0

Published by
F. A. Thorpe (Publishing)
Anstey, Leicestershire

Set by Words & Graphics Ltd.
Anstey, Leicestershire
Printed and bound in Great Britain by
T. J. International Ltd., Padstow, Cornwall

This book is printed on acid-free paper

To Caron, my own *boere meisie*,
best friend, lover, queen of the veldt,
from her *rooinek* buddy,
and for our girls, Laura Genevieve
and Margot Dorothy, sweethearts
of the rodeo, sho' 'nuff.

1

On its second day out of Portland, Oregon, the Northern Pacific Railroad's *Old Independent* hit trouble — again. Tackling the long pull-up into the foothills of the Bitterroot Range, Montana, she came screaming out of a long tunnel onto a curved gradient, her bell-stack belching black smoke and sparks as the engineer put on more throttle to take the gradient. The track curved into the mountain wall in a five-mile crescent, and peering out of his cab the oil-grimed engineer saw some distance ahead a barrier of rocks across the track.

'Bandits, by God!' he swore, hitting the brakes. As he did so there came from behind a stand of pines a bunch of masked riders, spurring their horses alongside the engine. Grimly he counted them, six, then raised his hand, gave two short whoops on the whistle, then six short blasts in quick succession. It was his last act in this world. A rider galloped alongside and shot him through the head with a short carbine. From his safe position in the woodpile the fireman saw the engineer fall from the footplate, and his own scream was drowned in that of the locked-on brakes.

Operating on a tried and trusted pattern the gang separated, leaving one man to hold the horses and keep an eye on the terrified young fireman. The first two desperadoes swung aboard the lead carriage, robbing the passengers as they worked through. No-one was safe. One fat patent-medicine salesman who tried to hide his diamond rings was gun-whipped to encourage the others, and it was amazing how quickly the more forgetful suddenly remembered that reclusive wallet, the overlooked gold watch-chain.

While one whooping bandit raced his mount up and down the length of the

2

train, firing into the air and shouting to the passengers to stay seated and not try anything, the remaining two rode swiftly to the caboose, wherein sat the conductor and the telegrapher, nigh on clutching each other with fright and wishing that the big safe in the corner would just walk out and give itself up without involving them. They did not confide their fears to the third occupant of the caboose who lay against one wall, but since he was confined at that moment to a polished rosewood coffin with all the brass trimmings, feet pointed skyward, arms across his chest, that was understandable.

The locked door splintered and the two masked gunmen were inside the caboose.

'Throw down yer guns, an' hand over the keys to the deposit box!' the tall guy in the tattered, confederate officer's greatcoat demanded.

'We ain't armed, and the safe key's in Chicago,' the conductor quavered. 'Been a change of company policy, since you boys been hitting us so hard.'

The other bandit cursed at the two men, then ordered them to lie face down on the floor while he turned his attention to the safe. Gun in hand the ex-confederate soldier looked over the inside of the caboose, his attention finally coming to rest on the coffin.

'Waal, lookie here,' he drawled, knocking playfully on the casket. 'We got company, Wes boy!'

'Dammit, Clyde,' the guy at the safe snapped. 'How many times I tell you, don't use names. Want every railroad dick in the country after us? Now we gonna have to waste these jaspers!'

'In a minute,' Clyde said absent-mindedly, as he bent over the casket, dismissing with a wave of his Colt the two railroad employees' assurances that they had heard nothing and, besides, they could be relied on to forget everything, you bet, gents.

Clyde was reading the name on the destination label, figuring it slow.

4

Book-learning wasn't his strong suit.

'Wes!' he finally yelled. 'Guess who we got in here? Come over here and get the laugh on this dude!'

Grudgingly Wes obliged, and leaning over he also figured out the name on the label.

'Tom Blood,' he pronounced. 'To be collected in Chicago by Hanson's, morticians, of . . . '

'Tom Blood!' shouted Clyde. 'That's got ter be *the* Tom Blood, the railroad's hired gun, the 'tec who's been chasin' us fer the past three month or so, plumb across three states! Looks like someone did us a favour!'

'Now ain't that somethin'?' Wes demanded, pulling down his mask to give a braying laugh, while pummelling Clyde's back.

It didn't occur to the two men as they laughed and whooped at the good news to consider why Blood's remains should be travelling east when there was plenty of good land back west to bury a man in, and they were having such a high old time, making such a din, that they did not at first register the gunshots which came from the carriage up front, where the party was just starting for the rest of their band. By the time it did sink in that things were not going according to plan, the fun had started for Wes and Clyde too.

It was in the second carriage that the other two hold-up artists had met the preacher and the lady. She was tall, willowy, with a long black veil and carrying a muff. Both men reflected fleetingly that she was sure wrapped up well against the mountain air as she swayed up the carriage towards them.

'Lady, take your seat and pass up your money and jewellery,' one of the men warned her, waving a gun at her.

'Oh,' she breathed in a cut glass limey accent, 'masked daredevils of the range! *So romantic!* Please don't shoot. I'll gladly give you my . . . trifles,' and she slowly began to unbutton with a kid-gloved left hand the high neck of her travelling-coat.

At the same time as she was beginning to disrobe, the preacher further down the carriage was struggling drunkenly to his feet, whiskey-bottle slopping in his pocket and a bible clenched under his armpit as he raised his free hand skyward, and begged the robbers not to shoot the young lady. A couple of women at the far end began to cry noisily. Things were getting a mite out of control for the two hold-up artists.

'Keep your brains above your waist and your eyes on the crowd while I collect,' snapped the other bandit, pushing past his transfixed partner, whose eyes were rooted to the soft white neck now being revealed, a froth of lace showing at the throat.

'It says in the good book, thou shalt not steal,' the preacher slurred in a whiskey-burnt southern accent. 'Let me read to you from the word that never dies, my son.'

'Brains' kept his eyes on the lace blouse that was now being unbuttoned. Such white, white skin; any time now an' I'm goin' to see her . . . what the hell? Black chest-hairs? With a gasp he made to bring his pistol up, just as further down the carriage the preacher opened his bible and pulled forth a forty-five from the hollowed-out depths of the book. Half-turned from the innocuous man of the cloth, the second bandit was not prepared for the point-blank impact of the bullet, and flew halfway across the carriage before he realized he'd been shot. As the gun's bark reverberated in the enclosed space the veiled lady pushed her right hand out of the fur muff she was carrying to reveal a snug little four-shot Sharps Presentation derringer she had been packing all along. No well-dressed lady should be without such a handy little accessory.

'Say goodnight to nursie,' the lady grated, in a voice markedly lower but still with a classy English accent, pulling the trigger to send a .30 calibre slug into 'Brains's' head just below his left ear. Maybe it would have been better for the outlaw if he *had* been carrying his brains in his pants as his recently deceased friend had suggested. That way the lady might have missed them first shot. The second shot she gave him as he fell floorwards was unnecessary, but made sure she'd missed nothing. Thorough work.

His drunken stagger forgotten now, the preacher skipped lightly across to the window of the carriage and pulling it down was just in time to loose off a couple of shots as the bandit who'd been left with the horses leapt into his saddle. He vaulted clean over his horse as the preacher's bullet took him in the back, rolling down the embankment in a cloud of dust.

'So perish the ungodly,' quoth the preacher, blowing the smoke from the barrel of his gun, and half a dozen passengers in the carriage replied, 'Amen.'

Back in the caboose a dead man called the play. Wes and Clyde had finished chortling once they heard the gunshots, and Wes made for the door. Behind them both men heard a creak, followed by a crash as the coffin lid hit the floor. They turned, dumbfounded, as the dead came to life. From the depths of the casket rose a tall, thin guy with cold blue eyes and thinning red hair. A thin beaked nose gave him the look of a pitiless bird of prey about to strike. The two gunsels were more occupied with what the liveliest corpse they'd ever seen was carrying, however. As he rose to a sitting position and uncrossed his arms, they found themselves looking down the business ends of a matching pair of Smith and Wesson No. 3s, Russian Model, best insurance a dead man can carry.

Clyde managed to squeeze off a wild shot, a bullet from his Colt caroming off the edge of the casket and burying itself in the silk lining. Blood fired twice with his right-hand gun at Clyde, a perfect target in the open doorway, in the same fluid movement bringing his left-hand gun round to train on a fatally slow Wes.

Clyde took both bullets in the abdomen and crumpled forward, falling across the outstretched, shaking forms of the telegrapher and the conductor, both still face down and clutching floorboards. Blood's second gun barked twice and Wes spun round, one slug in the guts and the other entering his heart and leaving a rose pattern of spreading crimson on the confederate grey of his coat. He squeezed off one bullet, which spent itself in the floor as he staggered back against a wall of the caboose and slid into a sitting position. His clouding eyes rested on the famous railroad detective he had feared for so long.

'Tom . . . ' he gasped and then died.

'Blood,' the man finished for him, stepping out of the casket and stretching.

'Blood,' said the telegrapher, a

pimply youth for whom the word callow seemed to have been invented. He looked at the corpse bleeding across his legs and was promptly sick.

'When you're finished,' Blood said to the telegraphist, nodding towards the conductor, 'take your friend here, round up some help, and get the track cleared. We'll drop off in Missoula with the bodies and see if the sheriff can put a name to any of them.'

The sound of drumming hooves broke into his speech, and he leaned over, took a Henry rifle from the casket and ran to the door. The last of the band had figured that the best defence was retreat and was making off at a lick.

Blood waited patiently, resting the rifle against the jamb of the caboose door and taking a sight not on the rider, but on the distant tunnel mouth. After a half a minute the white dust-coated back of the escaping owlhoot was outlined against the tunnel mouth and his back was plumb centre behind the bead of the Henry. Blood fired once, then raised his head to see the rider pitch forward onto the tracks. A ragged cheer came from the passengers who were hanging out of the windows. Something to tell the folks back East, by God.

'A good bag for a few minutes' shooting, old chap. The full three brace, what?' drawled the English 'lady' struggling manfully down the side of the train in the long skirt, 'her' veil thrown back now to reveal a dark-chinned, laughing man of twenty or so, an easy-going character whose deep, black eyes warned of a temper best to let lay.

'Good to see you, sweetheart,' said Blood, grinning. 'What *have* you been doing to that fetching outfit?'

The young Englishman tore off the skirt to reveal a more acceptable male form of dress below, travel-stained blue denim jeans.

'Whoowee!' shouted the preacher, coming up behind and offering the whiskey bottle round. 'Got the suckers, fer sure!' He took a pull and passed the bottle to Blood. 'Here y'go, Tom. Honey for the bears, boys! Ain't had so much fun since we set fire to granpaw!'

Blood took the bottle, and tilting it to the two men before him, toasted his partners, reflecting not for the first time that they made up a weird trio.

'Wild' Jack Storney, 'remittance man', youngest and most headstrong son of Sir John Storney of Storney Hall, Storney, Derbyshire, England. Sent out west in a hurry for killing a man in a duel over his sister's honour. Cheating the rope and having a whale of a time too. Living off a remittance from home and what the job paid. And with the bonus on these six bandits it would be paying well.

'Preacher' was Farley Bodeen, a Missouri poor white, though he'd have killed the man who said it, since the word 'trash' was always understood to follow that epithet. As

14

a boy of sixteen he'd seen farm and kin wiped out in the war within a war, the Kansas-Missouri border battles of the Civil War, had taken up his gun and long rifle against the Kansas 'Redlegs' who swept down upon lonely farms and settlements, killing, raping and burning indiscriminately. He had ridden against the likes of Jim Lane and his boys, with men such as Quantrill, Cole Younger, 'Bloody Bill' Anderson, throughout the Civil War and on into the Reconstruction of the South, a sharing out by the carpet-baggers that kept him riding and raiding. Until one day he'd said 'enough', and turned his horse's head west, earning his money the only way he knew how. Still in his twenties, an old man looked out from behind his eyes on a world filled with bad guys who needed his attention.

And Blood, Tom Blood, ramrod of the outfit, at thirty-something the old head who led them. Ex-U.S. Cavalry, ex-buffalo hunter, very much still a gunfighter and railroad detective who, like his companions, knew only one trade so tried to do it better, to someone else, before they did it to him.

Three men who went where any army could not go, who put their lives on the line, got results and kept the trains running on time. Some men. Some team.

Blood turned to his partners. 'Get the other dead ones in here,' he instructed, 'then let's get this loco rolling to Missoula. We got a timetable to run to on this railroad!'

2

At Missoula *Old Independent* snorted and hissed like some great, idling monster impatient to be unleashed while the young telegrapher and the conductor gingerly dragged the bodies of the failed hold-up artists onto the boards of the platform. A knot of idlers and two or three would-be passengers gathered at a respectful distance for a better view, while those passengers who had recovered from the shoot-out alighted and began to tell — and embroider — the tale for eager listeners. Farley and Jack busied themselves unshipping the outlaws' mounts, while Blood leaned against the clerk's office-cum-telegraph-shack and began patiently putting together a smoke.

Shoving through the crowd came a small, lame man, wearing a battered star on his grubby plaid shirt as his only badge of office. Apart, that is, from the strapped-down .44 Remington-Beals Army Model, low on his right thigh. The tin badge, the gun, and the name of Chad Layne gave three good reasons why badmen didn't stop over — alive — in Missoula too often.

'What y'got, Tom?' Chad asked, hitching up his pants and looking down on the massed ranks of the dead, laid out in a row before him.

'Let me introduce you to the gang who've been giving us all hell for the past six months or so,' Tom said, smoothing his smoke straight prior to gumming it down with his tongue.

'Waal, Momma allus said it was unwise to outstay your welcome any-place,' Chad drawled. 'Don't look much, do they, now?'

'They aren't at their best,' Blood agreed. He bent down and picked up one of the owlhoots' boots that had come off in the dragging and, avoiding a hole in the thin sole, he scraped a lucifer across the surface, lit his smoke, then tossed the boot onto the chest of its former owner.

'Recognize any of them?' he asked the sheriff. 'That one goes by the name of Wes, this one here' — he poked the nearest body with his boot — 'is called Clyde.'

Chad stroked his chin. 'Cain't say as I do,' he mused, 'though I hear tell the gang was led by a big, southern dude with a wall eye, similar to the one in the confederate coat yonder. Wes, you say? Nope . . . Shall we go through the Wanted fliers tergether? Might be in there.'

'That's why I brought them here, Chad,' Blood admitted. 'Same deal as usual. Me and the boys get the bonus from the railroad, but we split down the middle with you on any other rewards that are out, and you keep what you can get for their mounts and saddles. Farley and Jack are unloading them now. Don't think they'll amount to much — the mounts look like

19

they've been nigh on starved.'

'Rich men don't rob trains, Tom,' Chad observed, scrutinizing the corpses closer. 'I've sent my new deputy for the Wanted sheets. He'll be along directly.'

'New deputy? What happened to the old one?'

'Got shot an' quit,' said the sheriff. 'His own damfool fault. There was a dust-up in the saloon an' he tried to storm in an' settle it on his own. Should have gone round the back way and got the drop through the window, like I advised. No tellin' these kids, Tom, no tellin' 'em.' He grunted as he bent his game leg and squatted over the bodies.

'You search 'em for papers an' such, any leads on their names?' he asked.

'Jack shook them down,' Blood said. 'Found nothing but some nickels, a few dollar-bills and a bust mouth-harp. I've been too busy stretching to check. It sure was a tight fit inside that coffin.'

'Yer the first I heard complain,'

Chad replied, his fingers busy in the dead men's pockets. 'Nope, they seem clean, all ri . . . Hello, Miss Annie! Now, what have we here?'

From the last outlaw's vest pocket, the tall guy in the confederate coat, Chad drew out a small square of grubby paper.

'Something wrapped in it,' he observed, holding out a battered piece of dull, silver metal and shaking it so it rattled.

'Looks like a tin whistle,' Jack Storney said as he and Farley came up behind the pair. 'Sorry, Tom. Must have missed that.'

'Thet ain't no whistle,' said Farley, taking the object and rolling it in his palm. 'Thet's part of a musket-ball with a metal button wrapped around it. Seen a few sim'lar during the war. Middle of some battle, the ole minny-ball hits a guy spang in the middle of his chest, an' the button wraps around the ball, holds it tighter'n a bride hangs to her beau come the weddin' night. Saves the guy's life, fer sure, so he carries it as a charm from then on in, though it could as likely've ricocheted off and flown up his nose, taken his fool brain out. Looks like they's somethin' embossed on the button . . . ' He broke off and asked with a grave face, 'Which jasper did yer take this from?'

Blood indicated with a jerk of his head, and Farley bent down, looked close at the corpse's face.

'There's a note with it,' Blood said. He smoothed the paper out and began to read the crudely pencilled script.

'Dear cuzzin,' the note ran. 'Hope this is finding you as it leaves me. I am sendin my luck-peece to sho you that this letter is jake. I hear you are up to yer old tricks on the railroad up there, and holing out at Ed Gaits' place . . . '

'That lousy son of a bitch!' Chad Layne snarled. 'Guess it's time Mister Gaits got a visit.'

' . . . We are in the same line of

bisness down here in Paradise Valley,' Blood continued reading, 'only we are being paid to stop a railroad being bilt, and the guy who's payrolling it says we need more hands, so why not do yourself some good and git down here? It's like shooting fish in a barrel, cuz. We'll look out for you at the cave above the trail to Dos Hermanas, can't miss it. We'll be there every third day of the week for the next month or so. Joe and Nate are here and say hi, y'all. Your lovin cuzzin (tho' not kissing cuzzins!) Fletcher . . . ' Blood broke off and asked Farley, 'Do you know of this guy?'

'No, no,' Farley said hurriedly. 'Should I of?'

'No,' said Blood. 'It's just that you seemed mighty interested in the button and these bandidos are southerners. I just thought . . . '

'Hey, now,' Farley said, uncorking the whiskey bottle, 'we bred a hell of a lot of bandits in the south. 'Course, Tom, if we'd won they'd of been heroes, fightin' for freedom!'

Blood looked to Farley, then as he took the whiskey bottle seemed about to speak, when the young telegraphist stuck his head out of his booth and called to him, waving a yellow telegraph form.

'Telegram for Mr Blood!'

Blood took the pencilled form and read it over. Then he walked down to the group.

'Looks like we're getting our next job direct from the horse's mouth,' he told them. 'President of the whole shooting-works wants us in Fresno.' He handed the telegraph to Jack, who read it aloud:

'Hasland J. Coldwell to Thos. Blood, all stations north. Sir, your services required instantly stop Report Fresno soonest stop Bring companions stop Urgency stressed stop Am awaiting your attendance to instruct you personally stop Coldwell message ends.'

'The big cheese himself,' Chad Layne observed. 'What's cookin', Tom?'

'No idea, but it must be important,' Tom replied. 'Get your bags and stuff off the trains, boys. We're heading back down to Fresno on the next train through. The president requires our services!'

It may have been the haste to get their gear off the *Old Independent* which caused Farley to forget to hand back to Tom the silver button the dead outlaw had been carrying. He sure made it look that way as he stuck it absent-mindedly in his vest pocket and ambled onto the train. Blood, whilst pretending his attention was elsewhere, watched the southerner go, and wondered why, for the first time in their lethal business partnership, Farley Bodeen had lied to him.

Lies were not in short supply that afternoon in Missoula, for the next work the wide-eyed station telegraphist had was to send a hell of a long telegraph, dictated to him by a dandily-dressed, portly English dude. The man had alighted from the train when it first pulled in, and at the counter of the telegrapher's booth had finished writing an article he had started to pen way down the tracks, almost before the last outlaw had been stashed in the caboose. It was an 'eye-witness' account of the shoot-out, which if it lacked in truthfulness made up for it in sheer invention and colour. The telegrapher, who had come West after reading dime novels of similar hue, was enthralled as he tapped out every word on his telegraph key, to relay the thrilling story to the New York offices of a London newspaper, whose correspondent the portly liar was.

' . . . Little recked the bold Tom Blood, as he confronted the bandit chief who stood with pistols cocked and a Bowie knife between his teeth,' the Englishman dictated. 'Take this to Hell, you ruffian!' barked the brave, flint-jawed hero, his eyes blazing with manly anger. Drawing his pistol with a flourish he discharged it into the desperado's cowardly frame, and ere the southern rebel's last breath left his wretched body, our hero of the West had whirled and shot through a window to dispatch two more of the craven creatures who for so long had preyed upon innocent travellers. Meanwhile his brave compadres, confronted by more of the snarling villains swarming aboard the train . . . '

'I wonder,' said the newspaper correspondent, breaking off, 'if you would also be so good as to send a copy of this to the *San Francisco Mercury*? I have an arrangement there with the editor to report on my travels and any interesting incidents which occur along the way.'

'Oh, for sure,' the telegrapher assured him, impressed as all get-out. 'Gosh, you sure write a good story, mister.'

'One merely writes what one sees,' the journalist said, inclining his head modestly, 'but I pride myself that I do have a certain facility with words which appeals to my readers.'

3

It was a soft warm night, of the sort that comes to the valley in early summer, and as he rode home he whistled softly, if a little unsteadily, to himself. Hell, he'd had too much to drink tonight! Amy had been right to scold him. She hated the smell of drink on a man. He'd best be careful when he got back, too. If the old feller got wind that he'd been drinking . . .

He had to stay in with him if he was going to ask his daughter to marry him . . .

It was a shame about Amy. They weren't right for each other, never had been. It had been . . . convenient. Yeah, that was it. Convenient. And they'd both been lonely too. She'd see sense later on. That hadn't been a friendly parting. She'd said some pretty nasty things when he'd told her.

Well, she'd come around. Just as the old feller would when he told him his news. What news! He chuckled to himself at the thought. And he'd been responsible for finding it out! As for . . .

He had a vision of her smiling up at him as he told her. Later, of him asking her out. How could she refuse? He'd saved her old man, and her future. She'd look at him in a different light. She'd need a man around later on, and you bet the old feller would push his case for him. He chuckled again, breaking off when he saw the two figures loom up in the darkness, their horses barring his way. He squinted drunkenly into the dark as he heard them call his name, identify themselves.

'Oh, it's you guys. Kinda way outa town for this time of . . . '

The two shots took him completely by surprise, fired as they were by one of the riders who'd come up out of the darkness, smiling in a friendly manner

29

and, from six feet away, had shot him once in the chest and once in the belly.

His horse wheeled in alarm, careered down the slope at the side of the dirt road, and his body fell from its back and crashed lifeless into the brush.

'Sheeit!' swore one of the riders. 'Now we gotta go down there and drag him back up!'

4

The president of the Northern Pacific Railroad didn't meet just anyone, nor did he usually stir from his desk in his office back East. Hasland J. Coldwell came from an old Boston family, one of the first off the *Mayflower*, and the aristocratic hauteur of the Coldwell dynasty was once summed up by a Boston wit.

'They say of Boston,' he remarked to a visiting friend, 'that it is 'the land of the bean and the cod, where the Cabots speak only to Lowells, and the Lowells speak only to God.' Well, sir, let me tell you that if God wishes to speak to the Coldwells He has to make an appointment well in advance, and His business had better be important!'

Blood had never seen the man before, though legends about Hasland J. Coldwell abounded. It was said that he was miserly with money, shrewd in his business dealings, cold in manner and merciless with those who crossed him. Whatever was brewing, it had to be mighty big to bring the president of the whole railroad out West, and then send for them personally for a face-to-face, Tom thought as he and his companions picked their way over the ties in the Fresno railyard to where the presidential rail-car awaited them.

'Lookit the heathen Chinee!' Farley hissed as they neared the carriage. 'Speak softly ter him, boys!'

Lee Chi was indeed an impressive sight. Full six feet four and weighing easily two-forty pounds of solid muscle, he was Hasland Coldwell's conceit, a bodyguard and personal servant par excellence. His broad, handsome face betrayed no emotion, and he stood still as a statue on the railed platform of the car. He wore the traditional garb of a Chinese man, the silk tunic with wide sleeves and the black cotton baggy pants. Legs braced and arms folded with hands inside his sleeves, he barred their way, bowing courteously.

'No guns,' he informed them. 'You leave with me, please.'

'Y'can whistle *Dixie* for 'em!' Farley snapped. 'I don't even *bathe* without my hardware, y'damned dwarf!'

'Leave them be, Lee Chi,' a dry, whispery voice instructed the giant from inside the carriage. 'Bring Mr Blood and his companions inside, if you please.'

Lee Chi bowed and stepped aside. He kept his hands inside his sleeves. His left hand lightly rested on a wrist-sheath in which nestled a thin-bladed poisoned knife, and his other hand held a five-pointed throwing-star, a favoured weapon of the brigands known as lin kui of the northern forests of China, the 'forest demons' who spawned the ninja of Japan. A Kung Fu adept who had studied with the lin kui, Lee Chi accepted his master's ruling calmly. These three men would be no problem if they did prove hostile.

Inside the carriage were two men. One, a dark, good-looking man in his early thirties Blood did not recognize, but from all he had heard of Hasland J. Coldwell, then the old and wispy character, his scrawny neck protruding from a wing collar, keen-eyed and sharp-featured, reminding Blood of a hungry vulture, was the president of the whole shooting-works. He was seated at a large American Wooten desk of walnut that in a hundred years would fetch over a million dollars at a New York auction, but at the moment was earning its keep. From a honeycomb of pigeon-holes and drawers protruded maps, inventories, lists and logs of all sorts necessary to build and run a successful railroad, while on the panelled walls of this mobile office were large-scale maps. Coldwell rose behind his desk to his full height of five feet one, and offered a dry hand that felt like shaking a parchment stuffed with twigs.

'Gentlemen,' Coldwell whispered,

'thank you for responding so promptly to my summons. Allow me to introduce you to my brother-in-law, Edward Somersby of England. He is vice-president of the New Territories Pacific Railroad, my, ah, latest venture.'

Somersby did not offer his hand, and by the look of haughty disdain he threw their way, it seemed to the trio that he had scant regard for his brother-in-law's hired help.

'If you'd step over here I can better explain my predicament,' Coldwell continued, waving them over to a large wall-map which showed the North American continent. 'At present, we are linked with the East by means of my railroad, which takes a northern route to Chicago, and so onto the eastern seaboard. The southern states are not directly linked. Now, I intend to remedy that by building, with the approval of Congress, a new stretch of railroad from San Diego, California, to Santa Fe, New Mexico, where it will join up with existing railroad track taking it into the southern states, or turning north toward Chicago.'

'You started last year,' Blood said bluntly. 'What's the problem?'

'Perhaps my brother-in-law, whom I placed directly in charge of the operation, would like to explain,' Coldwell said, and stepped aside for the haughty young Englishman.

'You can follow a map, I take it?' Somersby drawled, and one sensed the atmosphere in the room grow colder at the implied insult.

'I guess I can keep up if you talk as slow as you are doing,' Blood said with a thin smile.

'Well,' said Somersby, tracing an elegantly manicured finger across the map, 'the planned route is from San Diego to the border town of El Centro, cross the Colorado River through low, fertile valley land to Phoenix, then from there follow the course of the Gila River till it turns north, head south-east, crossing into New Mexico, to Lordsburg, from there to Las Cruces, turning north and following the course of the Rio Grande through Albuquerque to Santa Fe, roughly 1,200 miles of track.'

'Let me guess the rest,' said Blood. 'All went reasonably well . . . '

'Apart from some of the steepest prices I've ever had to pay contractors per mile of track laid,' snorted Coldwell.

'Everything was going OK,' Blood resumed, 'until you got here.' He tapped the map where it was marked 'Paradise Valley'. 'Then some bandits tried to stop you building any further. Am I right?'

'How do you know that?' Somersby snapped.

In answer Blood unfolded the note found on the dead bandit.

'Took this off some hold-up artists we killed three days ago,' he said simply.

'Ah, yes,' said Coldwell. 'We have been reading of your exploits in the *San Francisco Mercury*.' He held out a copy of the broadsheet, and said drily,

'You are becoming famous, Mr Blood, you and your companions.'

Blood surveyed the screaming headline and the artist's impression of 'Dashing Tom Blood dispatching the Bandit Chief' and tossed the paper back onto the desk with a grunt of disgust.

'So, tell us about Paradise Valley,' he said.

'I can tell you more about that, and this note, than Edward here can, since he has been in charge of getting the railroad built and I have been handling, the, er, political side of it,' said Coldwell, rising to his feet and approaching the map. 'There is one man who opposes us building a railroad through the valley, and that man is behind the murderous attacks on us.'

'Hold hard,' said Tom, holding up a hand. 'Slow down, Mr Coldwell, and tell me about the valley first, then the guy you're up against. That way I'll get a clearer picture.'

Coldwell blinked at being interrupted,

then took a deep breath.

'You are quite right, sir,' he breathed. 'I was forgetting myself. A large part of my wealth is tied up in this railroad, and it galls me to lose so much money.' He took another, calming breath, then resumed, pointing with a bony finger to the valley on the map.

'This is Paradise Valley. It is almost two hundred and fifty miles long; to the north-east it runs into the foothills of the high mesa land beyond, and the Verde river descends, to wind down the valley roughly midway, running in a south-westerly direction. The whole valley is fertile and ripe for settling and farming. We have been given government land-grants of ten miles each side of the proposed track, as well as thirty-year loans for some of the cost, and that is how we will make our profits.'

'So what's to stop you?' asked Farley Bodeen.

'Someone is already sitting on the land,' said Coldwell, with an expression of distaste. 'A powerful rancher called Emory Hathersage. He has been running cattle on the open range down there for forty years. Opened the valley up himself and thinks he still owns it. If we go in with the railroad, he'll be ruined. Oh, there are already smaller spreads and a few piddling farms at the head of the valley, but Hathersage tolerates them to make it look as if he's open and fair. And one or two of those outfits have been hit by the gang that's operating down there, farms burnt out, innocent people butchered.'

'But most of the attacks are directed against the railroad, right?' Blood asked.

'That is correct. We have had rail crews attacked and men shot, trains derailed, bridges burnt down or blown up at night. It's holding us back, and time is of the essence.'

'Why?'

'Because there is another, rival railroad being taken through further north, and if that gets too much headway, then Congress will withdraw our land-grants, and we will end up with merely an expensive spur-line for the Northern Pacific, running down as far as the mouth of the Paradise Valley,' Coldwell told him. 'This is the era of the railroad, gentlemen. America is building railroads, and the railroad is building America. There is a great deal of money to be made in the game, but there is also a lot to be lost. And I do not intend to be a loser.'

'What can you tell me about the gang?' Blood asked.

'Incredibly, there's only six or seven of them,' Somersby said. 'Seem to be ex-confederate army, by the odd sighting and survivors' descriptions. Led by a big man with a patch over the right eye and a huge scar which runs through the eye, down his right cheek. Probably a sabre scar.'

'Any idea where they might be holed out?' Farley Bodeen asked, and Blood looked up quickly at the interest in his friend's voice.

41

Somersby sneered. 'Of course, they left us an address. We just haven't got round to calling on them yet!'

'It's obvious where they are,' Coldwell whispered in his dry-as-dust voice. 'They are holed up on the Hathersage ranch. He's their boss — it stands to reason. Mark my words, Blood. Watch Hathersage and you'll catch the gang.'

'So why don't you just get a whole bunch of men and ride in, search the place?' Blood asked.

'Because Hathersage has the ear of the governor of the territory,' Coldwell answered. 'He is making representations in Congress to get the land-grants in the Paradise Valley rescinded. It's my belief that he's using these acts of terror to slow us down while he does this, and to drive out the smaller settlers who've come in lately. When he's finished he'll be in a stronger position than ever. But mark my words,' Coldwell wagged a finger, and his voice became almost shrill, 'if you fail, Mr Blood, or tell me there is no other way, I shall send in a small army of gunfighters, and I shall wage war upon this Emory Hathersage.'

Blood mused for a while, looking at the map. He retrieved the note found on the dead outlaw, and studied the map again.

'Where's the cave below Dos Hermanas? he asked.

'Just here,' Somersby said, indicating a high range of mountains to the south-west of the Paradise Valley. 'It's a good place for a gang to hole up. Right at the mouth of the valley, within striking distance of the railroad.'

'Does anyone know you've sent for me?' Blood asked the president.

Coldwell shook his head. 'I kept it quiet,' he said. 'I didn't know whether you'd be available, or whether you would be prepared to take it on.'

'Well, what I reckon we could do is ride down to this Dos Hermanas and meet up with the gang,' Blood said.

'That sounds like an excellent idea,' Somersby jeered, and Blood flushed at his sarcasm. 'What then, ask them to kindly stop killing people and go home?'

'I reckon to make out that we're part of the gang they sent for, come on ahead to meet this jasper — what was his name — uh, cousin Fletcher?' He broke off and consulted the note again. 'Yea, cousin Fletcher . . . Say, Farley?'

'Tom?'

'D'you know of a southerner by the name of Fletcher?'

Bodeen shrugged. 'It ain't uncommon in the mountains to give a man his momma's maiden name,' he said.

'Oh,' Blood said, noting that Farley had evaded the answer. He turned again to Somersby with exaggerated courtesy and resumed his explanation of how he would contact the gang.

'So, we go down, meet the gang, and get in with them. Find out their camp, who's behind them, and then get the jump on them. Arrest them, or if they won't come peaceful, we kill them.'

'Hare-brained!' snorted Somersby.

'It's the best we've got,' Coldwell said, nodding to Tom. 'You know, a man could chase around that valley and the mountains for months and come nowhere near a whole army if you wanted to hide one away, Edward.'

'Rather a good plan, I'd say,' drawled Jack, who had not spoken before, and when Edward Somersby turned to look at him, nonplussed at hearing another cut-glass English accent, he extended his hand.

'Jack Storney, of Storney Hall, North Derbyshire, the Peak District, don't y'know,' he said, pumping the surprised Somersby's hand. 'You must be related to the Cheshire Somersbys, I presume?'

'Ah, distant cousins, I believe,' said Somersby. 'I'm surprised to find another English gentleman here, sir.'

'Oh, well, every family has its black sheep, eh, Somersby?' Jack said with a laugh. 'You are from . . . ?'

'Do you know Hampshire?'

'Oh, yes, then you will know the

Coke-Manderleys?'

'Good friends of my father's, Storney,' Somersby said shortly. 'Now, if we may resume?'

'Excuse me,' said Jack, waving a hand in a leisurely manner. 'I do prattle on so!'

'When can you be in Paradise Valley?' Hasland Coldwell asked.

'Well,' said Blood, considering. 'If you can send us and our mounts by train to this point here on the map tonight, and leave us at first light tomorrow, we can be at the cave by early morning, and that way we give folk less chance of getting wind of us being on our way.'

Coldwell nodded. 'It will be done, and no-one shall know that you are going there. I shall see to it. I appreciate your being ready. I do not need to stress that I am losing literally thousands of dollars for every day that this problem is unresolved.'

'I can understand your worrying . . . ' said Blood.

'I do not worry, Mr Blood. I pay other people to worry for me!' snapped Coldwell. 'One other thing . . . '

'Yes?'

'Keep an eye open for a young blackguard by the name of Chaney, Ben Chaney. He is an agitator, sir, and most probably in the employ of Hathersage also.'

'My brother-in-law and I have just returned from the Paradise Valley,' explained Somersby. 'The rail-gangs had ceased working, fearing that they would not be paid. The contractors hire the men, and provide the materials, and we pay the contractors per mile. Chaney had fomented agitation, telling the men that the railroad had gone bust and could not pay the contractors.'

'We delivered next month's payroll to the chief engineer, in the presence of the entire workforce,' snorted Coldwell, 'and I had the great satisfaction of personally sacking that damned Chaney. If you meet him, Mr Blood, please shoot on sight!'

'If I may suggest something?' Somersby interrupted, then turned to Blood with a haughty air. 'Whilst in the valley, you will report any progress made to the chief engineer, a man called Warren Keeler. He is in telegraphic contact with us, and we can pass on any orders through him. Understood?'

Blood's face grew as taut as a mask, his eyes turned to ice-blue, and he stared at the Englishman long and hard, till Somersby dropped his eyes and licked his lips nervously.

'Just so long as you understand that I handle this as I see fit, and take no orders from your Mr Keeler,' Blood said coldly, still staring straight at Somersby.

'I don't think anyone is disputing that you are your own man, Mr Blood,' Coldwell said, with a small smile at his discomfited relative.

'No?' asked Blood, and the challenge hung in the air, waiting for Somersby to take it up, if he were man enough.

'I still think that three men are not

enough to handle this problem . . . '
began Somersby.

'You've only got the one problem,'
said Blood. 'Seems to me we out-
number it three to one!'

'Two, Tom,' said Bodeen quietly. 'I
can't ride with you on this.'

5

Outside the carriage Farley said again, 'I'm sorry, Tom. I can't ride with you on this one.'

'It's because they're southern boys, isn't it?' asked Tom. Then added gently, 'The war's been over some time now, Farley. These guys aren't fighting for your side anymore.'

'Hang it, Bodeen, old feller! They're killers, and someone's got to stop them,' Jack added. 'Come now, ride with us.'

''Fraid I cain't, Jack,' Farley said, smiling apologetically. 'Guess I'll drift up Missoula way and see if Chad Layne wants a hand fer a while, smoking out that bandits' nest he aimed to do. I'll be up there when you're through, guys, if you need me again. No hard feelings, Tom?'

Tom took the proffered hand and gripped it hard.

'None at all,' he said. 'Take care, partner. Be seeing you.'

Tom and Jack watched as the young southerner crossed the ties to where their horses had been brought off the train from Missoula and began to saddle his roan.

'A dollar to diamonds he don't head north,' Blood said quietly to Jack.

'What makes you think that?'

'Because I reckon he's got friends down there in Paradise Valley, among those bandidos. D'you notice how strange he was when we found that note on the dead guy, the one signed Fletcher?'

'Sorry, missed that,' said Jack.

'Kids play a game,' said Blood, taking out a sack of tobacco and papers from a vest pocket, offering Jack a roll. 'Button, button, who's got the button? You got it, Jack?'

'Button? Oh, the . . . '

'Yeah, the button with the musket-ball in it. You got it?'

'No, I thought . . . Farley was

holding it when the telegraph came for you!'

'That's right,' said Tom. He shook tobacco onto a wheatstraw paper, rolled a smoke and sealed it with his tongue. 'And he's still got it. And now he's going to take it down to Paradise Valley to give back to his murdering friend. The one he don't know, by the name of Fletcher.'

'You don't think Farley would throw his lot in with the gang, do you?'

'No, I don't. The guy's straight,' Blood said. He struck a lucifer and lit his smoke, squinted over to where Farley was cinching down his saddle. 'He's going to do something far more dangerous, is my guess. He's going to play fair with them, for old time's sake, and that could get us all killed.

'And what was all that back there,' Blood asked Jack, jerking his head backwards at the president's carriage, 'with the Somersby dude?'

'He's not what he pretends to be,' said Jack, flicking away his smoke.

'His accent is false. An American wouldn't spot it, but now and then one can discern a London twang to it. And those families I mentioned, the Somersbys of Cheshire, the Coke-Manderleys of Hampshire?'

'Yeah?'

'There's no such families of any social standing in those counties,' Jack said. 'I made them up. Yet he pretended to know of them.'

'So what does it matter?'

'Maybe not much,' said Jack. 'But being an English gentleman, part of the aristocracy, is being part of an exclusive club, Tom, and one member can tell another. I'm no snob. I'm just telling you that that man back there is pretending to be something he's not. He's not 'top drawer', as we say back home. Now, he may have done it just to marry into the Coldwell family. Or he may not.'

Blood nodded thoughtfully. 'Well spotted, Jack. It's as well to know he's playing his own corner. Now, let's get moving. We've got an appointment in Paradise!'

* * *

Blood was right about Farley. Once out of the rail-yards he turned the roan's head south, picking out the dusty trail that led from Fresno to Paradise Valley and setting a steady pace. It was going to be a long hard journey, several days' travelling, and he knew that he couldn't be there before Tom and Jack would. But somehow he guessed, if he knew the people they were all heading towards, they wouldn't be waiting in the cave at Dos Hermanas when the two railroad 'tecs arrived. With luck, if he pushed himself and his mount, he could be there before the killing started. And maybe he could stop it.

6

They travelled through the evening and all night, in a train made up of one carriage with a stove and coffee-pot and a boxcar behind for their horses. Blood stripped his rifle, a Henry sixteen-shot repeater, known by the confederates as 'that damn Yankee rifle that's loaded on a Sunday and fires all week'. Checking the rest of his insurance, he also cleaned and oiled his Smith and Wessons, then turned in and slept in his roll on the floor of the rocking wagon, while Jack stared for long hours out of the window, whistling tunelessly and smoking, watching the coastal, fertile country turn to semi-desert, then become lush again as the train began slowly to rise into the uplands that led to Paradise Valley. Finally, Jack slept too.

When the light in the sky was a

pearly grey Tom shook Jack awake.

'Train's stopped,' he said, placing a tin mug of hot, strong coffee in his hand. 'Time to ride, feller.'

'Ye Gods!' yawned Jack. 'I dreamed I was fox-hunting, back home in good old Derbyshire.'

Within ten minutes they were astride their mounts, watching as the wood-burner reversed back up the track, showering sparks and smoke from its high stack as it gained speed. In the far distance, black against the early morning sky, the two riders could faintly see the twin pillars of Dos Hermanas, the Two Sisters, as the first Spanish missionaries called them, rising up against the range which formed the north-western mouth to Paradise Valley.

'Time to go hunting,' Blood said, spurring his black gelding on, searching out the trail that led towards their quarry.

'Tally-ho,' murmured Jack contentedly. They rode silently for several hours, paused to rest up a while and eat, then pressed on, each man alert, rifle held before the saddle, loose in its scabbard, scanning the trail for any sudden challenge. Of the cave at Dos Hermanas they could see nothing, since the lower flanks of the rocks were obscured by cotton-wood and blue oak, giving way to spruce and ponderosa pine as the trail steadily climbed.

They saw the figure on the rock when they were some two miles away from it. Whoever it was made no attempt at concealment, and both Jack and Tom approached warily, having untied the thongs which held their rifles snug. As they got close they saw that it was an Indian, sitting cross-legged, a blanket thrown loosely around his shoulders. His long hair was held back by a red bandana. Beneath the blanket he wore rawhide leggings and a store-bought coat.

'Apache,' Blood murmured, reining his horse in.

The Indian rose from the rock and

held a hand up as a sign of peace, then slid down and walked towards them. As he came close to their mounts they saw by his lighter skin and blue eyes that he was a 'breed', half white, half Indian, still young, in his late twenties.

'You be Tom Blood and Jack Storney?' he enquired.

Blood raised his eyebrows to Jack. 'Some secret, huh?' he asked, then to the Indian, 'How do you know our names? Who sent you?'

The Indian ignored the questions. 'If you keep on this trail you're gonna be jumped,' he said. 'The sheriff of Eden and one of his deputies are waiting back of the rocks where the trail narrows, 'bout two mile on.'

'And how do we know you're not lying to us, old sport?' Jack asked pleasantly. 'What if you are trying to trap us yourself?'

The Indian shrugged. 'You can follow me and see,' he said. 'Or you can keep on and get killed. Choice is yours.'

'I like to know who I'm talking to,' said Blood, 'and who told you our names?'

'I'm Billy Free,' the breed told him. 'As for your names, the whole town of Eden knows you're coming. I got close enough to the sheriff and his deputy to hear that you're who they're waiting for. You want to see? I can take you to where you can get the drop on them, Tom Blood.'

Tom looked at Jack, then he too shrugged. 'Why not?' he said. 'We'll come with you, but you ride just in front of us, and stop if I tell you.'

Billy nodded, then walked round the rock he had been sitting on to where a pinto cow-pony was tethered. He leaped into the saddle and urged the pinto up the side of the trail, between the trees. The game little pony began to climb, followed by Blood and Storney. Soon they reached a smaller trail which paralleled the other, and Billy Free turned the pony onto it and picked his way slowly along it. After a mile

59

or so he stopped and tied his mount up, motioning for the others to do the same.

'We'll go on foot now,' he said, then looking down at his own, soft moccasins and at the others' boots, 'and be quiet. We come out right above them. They mustn't hear us.'

'Now hold hard,' Jack said, placing a hand on Billy Free's arm. 'I want to hear why the sheriff of Eden should want to kill me.'

Billy shrugged. 'I don't know,' he said. 'But you'll know more when you see inside the cave.'

'And why should you be trying to help us?' Blood demanded.

'When I was a boy,' Billy Free said, staring into Tom Blood's eyes, 'the white soldiers came to my village, up here in the mountains. They killed my father. He was Indee, which means of The People, Apache. He raised me after my mother, a white woman — the only wife he ever took — died. When she died, he cried for many days.

They killed him like an animal, killed women, babies even. A soldier saw me, lifted me on his horse. 'Billy, you're a white boy. You're free now,' he says to me. So they took my Indian name and called me this. Billy Free Hah! They brought me to an Indian school. I was starved, beaten, made to learn your ways. I ain't been free since.'

Blood dropped his gaze. He had been a soldier. He knew the truth of what the 'breed was saying.

'When I was a man I went back to my people, to our ways. There are still some of us free, up here in the mountains. If the railway comes, they will not be allowed to live there. The railroad will kill the valley, will invade the mountain with smoke and noise. The gaan, the spirits that live on the mountain along with the wind, will be troubled.'

'Hey,' Blood said, 'we haven't come to stop the railroad going through, Billy.'

'No,' Billy said. 'But I've fasted and

prayed to the gaan. I saw that two men would come, would help. You may be those two. Maybe not. All I do now is just keep you alive. It could be you are in with the sheriff and all the others who want to sell our land, steal our lives. If so, I am in danger. If not, I may help you more, later. All I say now is don't believe what the sheriff tells you. There's much here in Paradise that isn't as it seems at first. Now, follow me.'

He took a carbine from his saddle-roll, indicated that they should bring their rifles, then led them along the narrowing path that wound around between trees and rocks till they came out onto a ledge that looked down on the main trail. To their left they could see where it ended at the black mouth of a large cave below the twin stacks of Dos Hermanas. Below them the trail had to narrow to pass between two outcrops of boulders, and on the flattened tops of the rocks lay two men, bellies down, rifles extended before them, waiting in ambush for whoever rode unsuspecting towards the cave. Billy pointed to the far distance where could faintly be discerned a small cloud of dust. When Blood shook his right finger in the sign for 'what?' Billy put his own finger to his lips and withdrew, beckoning for them to follow him out of sight and hearing of the men below.

'That's a posse from Eden,' he told them. 'The sheriff has sent them out in a wide loop, scouring for men who took the payroll from the rail-camp last night. I watched this morning, saw the sheriff send them off with one of his deputies and then he and his other deputy came straight here. They wanted to kill you first and make it look as if they thought you were bandits going to the cave. When you have the sheriff and his deputy disarmed, fire shots and the posse will come. They are the townspeople, shopkeepers and such who'll profit from the railroad, but they are honest people and aren't in on this plan to kill you. You'll be safe when they are here.'

'So what's in the cave?' Jack asked.

'I'm not sure,' said Billy. 'I know some of what's there, but look for yourself, and don't believe what the sheriff tells you.'

He turned and made his way back along the track, leaving them on their own once more.

'Come on,' said Blood to Jack, pulling his hat down hard. 'Let's introduce ourselves to the sheriff.'

7

'Move and you're meat!' Blood shouted, and the two men on the rock below jerked with surprise, then stiffened.

'Easy now,' the gunman advised them. 'Bring your hands back and away from your rifles. Leave them lay, bring your hands further back, keep them clear of your gunbelts, now get them up behind your necks and clasp them. You try anything you'll be breathing through your backs. OK, now my partner's going to come and take your guns. Don't try it, it just ain't worth it.'

Pistol in hand, Jack jumped down onto the rock. One man moved slightly and Jack landed fair and square in the small of his back with one knee and with his free hand drove his head down into the rock, muffling the 'oof' of breath he'd driven out. Jack knocked the rifle off the rock, snatched the pistol out of the man's belt, patted him down, then did the same for the other.

'Now, you bushwhacking scum,' Jack said pleasantly, 'let's have you down off the rock, nice and easy, and line up with your hands behind your necks. OK, Tom.'

'Listen, mister,' the oldest of the two, a balding, overweight guy with a cast in his left eye, said. 'Did you call him Tom?'

'He did,' said Blood, sliding down to join his partner. 'What's it to you?'

'There's been a big mistake,' the man said, lowering his hands. 'Guess I owe you an apology . . . '

'You move those hands down any further,' Blood snapped, 'and you won't have time to say sorry! Hoist them!'

'I'm the sheriff round here,' the man spluttered. 'The name's Jake Dawson. This here's m'deputy, Mort Green. Y'can see our stars on our shirts, look!'

'Don't shoot, Blood,' pleaded Mort

Green, a weaselly little character with a toothbrush moustache. 'He's telling the truth. We didn't know you were the railroad 'tecs!'

'Nothing personal, you were just going to shoot the first fellows who came along, eh?' asked Jack, collecting up the lawmen's hardware.

'No, it ain't like that,' Dawson said. 'See, there's been a hold-up at the rail-camp last night. The chief engineer shot one of the bandits, and I got a posse up. Rest of the posse's out there somewhere. We searched this way and found a couple of dead guys in the cave and some of the bank-wrappers off the money they took. Looks like it's that gang you're after. So we staked the place out in case the rest of the gang came back.'

'OK. Turn around slow, touch the rock with your faces and spread your hands above you,' Blood instructed.

'Honest, that's how it was,' Mort Green quavered, nigh on crying with fear of the guns pointing at him.

Were he and Dawson going to be executed? He'd heard of Blood, and his reputation was mean with a big M. Maybe he'd shoot them just for being inconvenienced. Oh, shit, why did he ever listen to Jake? These guys were professionals, for Chrissake. You don't bushwhack these kind of . . .

When the shots rang out both Dawson and Green nearly had accidents. The relief of finding that they weren't dead, that Blood had merely been signalling to the distant posse, almost made Green faint. A distant salvo of shots from the posse told him that help was coming. Oh, thank you, God, he prayed, and then, if I ever get a chance, I'll kill that cold-eyed son of a bitch and his limey friend.

'Now, me and my friend here's going up to look in the cave,' Tom told them. 'Dawson, you come with us and show us. Green, you keep staring at that rock and don't either of you get any ideas. You may be the law round here, or you may have taken those stars off some sorry guys who got too slow. We'll find out later. For now, take it easy and there's only your pride gets hurt.'

Jack blew Green a loud kiss and followed Tom and the sheriff up to the cave, but once in there his easy smile left his face.

The cave was large and dry with a high roof, and the mouth and some holes higher up let in a lot of light. Enough to see that on the sandy floor lay two young men. That was all they had going for them, however, since both were dead, with gunshots to their chests and abdomens. Close by one body lay an open cash-box, empty, and scattered around the floor were paper strips used to wrap bundles of notes and bearing the title 'Western Bank, San Francisco' on them.

'Know these guys?' Blood asked Dawson.

'Sure,' the sheriff replied. 'This guy's Ben Chaney. He was a ganger on the railroad till three days ago. Coldwell personally fired him for stirring the men up. Other stiff is Dan Johnson, was foreman on the Hathersage spread. Looks like these fellers were part of the gang we been hunting, there was a disagreement over the share-out, and these two got each other in the shoot-out. Less o'course that damned Indian did for 'em both.'

'What Indian?'

'Halfbreed called Billy Free. He and these guys and another youngster by the name of Henry Boyd, surveyor for the railroad, were surprised by the chief engineer last night. He caught 'em at the strong-box in his wagon, shot one as they escaped with the money. So, we're looking for Free and Boyd. Bet they gone to join the rest of the gang. Want my advice, Blood, you'll search the Hathersage ranch. That's where they holed out, I reckon.'

Just then came the noise of horses on the trail below, and the sound of voices hailing them. Blood glanced out of the cave.

'Looks like some of the posse's here,'

he said to Jack. 'Take the sheriff down and greet them while I have a look around.'

When Jack returned without the sheriff, Blood was bent over the body of Ben Chaney.

'Look at this,' he said to Jack, indicating the dead man's vest.

'Powder-burns,' Jack said, then looked across the cave at the body of the other man. 'But if Johnson shot him, then he would have had to be a hell of a lot nearer.'

'Exactly,' Blood nodded. 'Now come look at Johnson.' He took Jack over to where the young foreman was lying on his back, staring sightlessly up at the cave roof. Blood pulled open the man's shirt to reveal his naked chest.

'Look here. Know what that is?' he asked, pointing to a red flush on the chest, then a paler area on the man's belly.

'No,' said Jack.

'It's called 'lividity',' Tom told him. 'Someone dies, the blood drains down

71

to the lower parts of the body that aren't in contact with a hard surface like the ground, or pressure from tight clothing. Usually, the body's lying face up, so the blood drains to the back of the neck, the small of the back and the thighs.'

'But he's lying on his back,' said Jack.

'That's right,' nodded Blood. He rolled up Johnson's trousers and showed that the legs were flushed with blood too. 'Lividity starts to show after three to four hours, and it's at its fullest after twelve. This is pretty well on, so it's my guess that this guy was shot around twelve hours ago, say late evening. He was killed somewhere else and then slung belly down, over a horse, maybe toted around for quite a while till they'd decided what to do with him, then he was brought here and his body arranged to make it look like he was shot in the cave. Look at his boots.'

'The toes are all scuffed and torn,'

Jack said, examining Johnson's boots. 'He's been dragged a distance.'

'Yeah, and look at the soil in the tops of his boots,' Blood said, pulling out a few pinches of soil that had been dragged into the wide boot-tops and caught in the folds of his pants. 'What colour's that?'

'Red,' said Jack. 'But the soil's yellow sand in here, and almost black outside.'

'There's nothing like that around here,' agreed Tom. He bent close to the corpse's mouth and sniffed. 'I can smell whiskey on him. He'd been drinking before he was shot.'

'So it looks as if they jumped him when he was drunk and then dragged him to a horse and toted him here,' said Jack.

'This is the clincher,' said Tom, showing Jack the fatal wound in Johnson's chest. 'Look how the blood from the wound's soaked into his shirt, not around the wound, or below it, but *above* it. The blood's run upwards, which shows he must have been slung over something face down either before he was dead or shortly after.'

'What about the other guy?' asked Jack.

'I think he was shot right here,' said Blood, getting up and walking over to Chaney's body. He rolled the body over, pulled up the corpse's shirt and showed how lividity was normal for a man who'd died in the position Chaney was lying in.

'There's another point,' said Blood, rolling the corpse's head to one side. 'When he fell he hit the floor with the back of his head, then rolled so the side of his face was grazed. Look, he's bled from the scratches as he died. There's sand from the cave floor in the grazes too.'

'So this whole scene in here was arranged as a tableau,' Jack said slowly. 'But who by, and who for?'

'It's my guess that the sheriff and his guys did it,' said Blood. 'And if Chaney was shot here, he was probably in on it too. Maybe the sheriff and his deputies figured that if Chaney'd got the poke from the railroad then he'd outlived his usefulness, and he would have known too much to just let go. He could have talked.'

Jack nodded. 'Give a dog a bad name and hang it — or shoot it in this case,' he said. 'So, this is the picture: Chaney and the others shoot Johnson, tote him around for a while, then bring him here. Then the others shoot Chaney, leave these bankwrappers and the cash-box, and wait for us. Right?'

'Right,' said Blood. 'I reckon that whoever arranged this planned to kill us too and stick our bodies in here, make it look like we'd come across the gang and they'd killed us. Maybe Johnson here was killed to make it seem as if that rancher, Hathersage, is in on it.'

'So we die, the pay-roll disappears, Hathersage is implicated, Hasland J. Coldwell sends in the guns against him, and there's a small war between Hathersage and his supporters and the railroad's guns. That way the building of the railroad's held up again,' Jack said, thinking aloud.

'Maybe,' said Blood. 'One thing's for sure — like Free said, the sheriff isn't to be trusted. We'd do well to keep him close to us, and watch him, see what he does next. For now, let's just play along.'

Just then came the sheriff's voice from down on the trail.

'Blood! Hey, Blood! Come on down, will ya?'

Tom smiled thinly. 'Sounds like our sheriff's got his nerve back now he's got the posse behind him,' he said. 'Come on, let's go meet the good townsfolk of Eden.'

8

Down on the trail were a score or so of men, nearly all on horseback save one large, dandified old guy in a frock-coat, pinstripe trousers and sporting a white goatee beard who had ridden in on a light buggy.

'So that's what stirred the dust up out there,' Blood said with a smile.

The old man hailed Tom and Jack, and, leaning down, extended a pudgy hand that was still surprisingly strong in its grip.

'Allow me to introduce myself,' he said, with the air of one conferring a favour. 'The name's Crawford Chilton, late chief reporter with the *New York Journal*, now sole owner and editor of the local paper, the *Eden Irregular Times*, sir. I understand that I have the pleasure of addressing Mr Tom Blood, pistolero extraordinaire, and this will be one of your, ahem, 'sidekicks' is, I believe the expression? Mr Bodeen or Storney?'

'Jack Storney,' said Jack, extending his hand also.

'I was given to understand that you were a trio,' said Chilton, looking around.

'Mr Bodeen had to pass on Paradise,' said Jack.

'He is the loser, sir. Came this way myself for my health, ten years ago. Never regretted it. God's country, sir, God's country.'

'How the blazes did you know we were coming?' Jack asked bluntly. 'It was supposed to be a secret.'

In answer the editor put a hand inside his frock-coat and withdrew a copy of yesterday's *Eden Times*, bannered 'Special Edition', bearing the headline 'Heroes of Missoula Due in Paradise'. With a flourish Crawford Chilton passed the paper to Blood, and once again Tom read the highly embroidered account of the shoot-out on the train. Even the sketch of the 'Dashing Tom Blood dispatching the bandit chief' was there.

'The whole thing was telegraphed to me by a friend who edits a San Francisco newspaper,' Chilton told them. 'We have a reciprocal agreement to send each other topical stories.'

Blood shook his head and handed the paper back angrily. Because of some fool journalist on that train his edge on the gang had been lost. Now everyone in the valley knew he was here. Dammit all to hell, he thought.

'Think we could have our guns back now, Mr Blood?' The sheriff's surly tones broke into Blood's thoughts.

'Oh, sure; sorry, Dawson. Jack, the guns. Listen, sheriff, no hard feelings, huh?'

'None here, Blood.' The look on the sheriff's face, and on the weaselly deputy's, told him differently, and it was not lost on Crawford Chilton either.

'I do believe you've made yourself an enemy there,' Chilton said to Blood as the sheriff hailed his other deputy, a squat, shambling bear of a man and with another of the posse they carried the two dead men out of the cave, to load on the back of Chilton's buggy.

Blood shrugged. 'Guy's lucky he's not dead,' he said. 'We had him cold. All we hurt was his dignity.' He leaned back against the buggy, rolling a smoke while Jack went off after their horses.

'Most of the posse will be pleased you made him look a fool,' said Chilton. 'He's not as well liked as the old sheriff, Bob Croft.'

'What happened to him?' Blood asked, striking a lucifer on the wheel rim.

'He was killed,' said Chilton.

'Who by?'

'An unknown assailant. Found dead on the outskirts of town one night with a single rifle-shot to the head. Looked like someone laid up in a grove of trees, waiting for him going home. He had a little spread outside of town, used to go home most nights to his wife. That was when the town was nice and quiet, just before the railway got here.'

'How long before the railway got here?' Blood asked.

'Oh, about a year ago. We all knew it was coming; most of us were for it, you know. Except Bob Croft. And then, when he went and we were looking for a lawman, along came Jake Dawson, Mort Green and that other creature of his, the animal they call Sam Collins. He's a nasty piece of business,' Chilton said, almost shuddering.

'And they were voted in as sheriff and deputies?' Blood asked idly. 'No-one opposed them?'

'Well, no-one liked to when they came so highly recommended,' Chilton answered.

Blood broke off while the two bodies were loaded and covered with a tarpaulin. Jack brought his horse and both the gunmen and the posse of townsfolk mounted up and headed for Eden. When they had travelled a while, Blood edged his horse alongside the buggy and asked the editor, 'Who recommended Dawson and his boys as the law in Eden?'

'Thought you would have known,' said Chilton. 'None other than the president of your railroad, Mr Blood. The great Hasland J. Coldwell!'

Blood said nothing, but rode on deep in thought. After a few minutes Crawford Chilton looked around to make sure he wasn't going to be overheard, then said, 'How's that sit with you, Tom Blood?'

'What?'

'Well, I guess you could call it the professional interest of a good newsman, or just an old man's nosiness, but whatever is happening here in the valley, it strikes me that the sheriff and his two deputies are involved. How do you feel to find out that maybe your boss is involved in these killings?'

'Coldwell pays me, but he doesn't own me,' Blood replied shortly. He thought for a few seconds, then said, 'I can't see Coldwell being involved. He sent me down here to stop the killings, didn't he?'

Chilton smiled and said, 'Maybe you and your young friend were intended to be sacrifices.'

'Meaning?'

'Well, if you were killed, then Coldwell could put pressure on his political friends who've been campaigning so successfully for him in Washington to have the army sent in, Hathersage driven out and all the land would be offered to the railroad to dispose of to settlers. We are talking of millions of dollars of prime real-estate, my friend. A man like your employer would stoop pretty low to gain such a prize, and what would a few more lives matter when so many have been lost already?'

'Sounds a little far-fetched to me,' Blood said. 'Coldwell wrecking his own railroad, killing his own people.'

'Well,' said the editor, 'there's been

a lot of folk killed around here who were just tending to their own affairs, and maybe I'm sticking my neck out too far, like a chicken on the block, but that's a newspaperman's way, to meddle in other's affairs. I'll tell you this for free.' Here he jerked his thumb back over his shoulder, to where the sheriff and his deputies slunk behind them like coyotes cheated of their prey. 'Those blackguards meant to kill you today, and whatever's going on here in Eden, they are in it up to their eyebrows. Watch your back from now on, Tom Blood. Watch your back.'

9

The first white men to see the area had named both the town and the valley after struggling up, half burnt-alive from the hell's-anvil heat of the Sonoran Desert. They were part of a combined military expedition to capture the fabled cities of gold for Spain and a religious mission to claim the souls of the heathen Indian for God. Close to exhaustion they chanced upon the mouth of a lush, well-watered upland valley which stretched out further than their eyes could see.

'Surely, Father, we are close to Paradise!' exclaimed a soldier to one of the Jesuit priests.

'Then we are in Eden, my son,' the black-robed priest said, 'for Eden stood just outside its gates, did it not?'

The priests and the soldiers established a mission and a presidio, a barracks, and the place was named Eden, the valley beyond, Paradise, and though the Spanish had long since gone by the time that Blood and Storney rode in, the town of Eden still retained some of its Spanish flavour, fighting a losing battle against the timber-fronted stores which jostled the white adobe buildings and, at the far end of the main drag, a railway depot which screamed 'Yanqui!', and from where shining rails wound off to despoil the valley which the simple Spanish soldier had seen as heaven.

The two railway detectives split off from the posse, and on the advice of Crawford Chilton made their way to the smaller of the two saloons in town, the Cattleman's Rest, where they booked adjoining rooms and baths. They had barely time to drop their saddlebags on the floor of their rooms, however, when there came a peremptory knock on Blood's door, and without waiting to be invited a tall, elegant man in his late fifties with a mane of long, silver hair swept in.

To be met by the business end of a cocked Smith and Wesson No. 3, Russian Model, pushed up close to his nose.

'Now, don't even breathe,' Blood advised the man. 'Arms out, level with your shoulders, and walk slowly back to that wall. Blink and you're dead, stranger!'

Jack had pussyfooted in behind the tall guy and he reached under the long black frock-coat and whipped out a silver-handled Colt, threw it across the room onto the bed, then kicked the door to behind him and locked it.

'This is outrageous!' the fancy dude spluttered.

'Sure is,' Blood said calmly, patting the man down to make sure he had no other weaponry concealed. 'You rent a room for two dollars a day and half the town seems to think it has a right to stampede through, huh, Jack?'

'I don't have one in my room,' Jack

grinned, then stuck his own gun at the back of the stranger's head and cocked it loudly. 'I advise you to state your business as a matter of some urgency, friend!'

'I am here as the representative of your employer,' the old guy shouted, his voice going up a notch in fear. 'The name's Warren Keeler, and I happen to be chief engineer of this damned railroad. My God! You lunatics nearly killed me!'

Blood shrugged as he stashed his iron. 'You walk into my room without an invite,' he said, 'and you can expect a window in your waistcoat. Now, what can we do for you, Mr Keeler?'

'Well, take your time, walk around town, see the sights, settle in for a day or two, then come see me, why not?' said Keeler sarcastically. 'I'll tell you why I'm here, Blood. I want you to haul your asses over to the Hathersage ranch and start looking for that gang and the money they took off me last night!'

'First point,' said Blood patiently, 'I'll go visit Hathersage when I think fit. Second point, Keeler, I do not take orders from you. You are my messenger-boy to Hasland J. Coldwell, and if you don't believe me just haul *your* ass, telegraph the guy and check. Savvy?'

Keeler took it and swallowed hard, not speaking, but it was clear by the pained look on his face that he was having a job digesting it.

'Now,' said Blood, 'you can help me by telling us about the stick-up. What happened?'

'About ten o'clock last night,' Keeler said stiffly, 'I was in the far end of the rail-wagon that serves as sleeping-quarters for me and the surveyor, young Boyd, and the planning and chart office. I was asleep, but a noise awoke me. Boyd had been away on a surveying trip, and I hadn't expected him to be coming back that night. I went to investigate and found him and Chaney in the office. They had the cash-box out of the safe. I had that day taken receipt of a month's pay-roll, and it was in the cash-box they were stealing. I challenged them and they made off into the night. I pursued them, firing — I think I hit one man, for we found blood on the ground later — and saw that they were in the company of Billy Free and that foreman from the Hathersage ranch, Dan Johnson . . . '

'Why wasn't the office locked?' Blood asked.

'It was,' Keeler answered. 'But, as surveyor, Henry Boyd had a key, and he also had a key for the strong-box. There are confidential reports, and the original survey is also kept in there, away from prying eyes.'

'You say Boyd often went on trips away from camp?' Blood asked.

'Yes. That was his job. To follow the original survey and to make a more detailed one, lay out the course of the track we were building,' Keeler answered with ill-disguised impatience.

'And he'd been out the night before?' Blood asked.

'Yes, he had been gone for three nights. I wasn't expecting him back.'

'Didn't you think it was dangerous, with this gang in the valley?'

Keeler snorted. 'It only proves the young thief was in with them, and, in my opinion, how they were kept apprised of any moves against them.'

'Who usually went with him, to help with the surveying equipment?' Blood asked.

'That damned insolent Ben Chaney,' Keeler said. 'He and Boyd were as thick as thieves.'

'The gun,' said Blood. 'Did you have it in the room or pick it up?'

'Gun?'

'Sure. The gun you shot one of the thieves with. You say you were asleep. You went in and shot at them. Now, was it in your wagon or the office? Why didn't they shoot at you when you walked in?'

'I sleep with the gun near my bed,'

Keeler snapped. 'I walked in with it held out before me, and they ran like the cowards they are. Now . . . '

'It must be fairly usual for the surveyor to use the office late in the evening,' Blood said. 'Why didn't you think he had come back? Why were you so suspicious?'

'Because of the money in the strong-box,' Keeler exploded. 'Now, I'm sick of being questioned as if I was involved. Get out there, find the men responsible and bring the money back. Find either and you will find the gang, is my opinion. I am off to report my reservations about your suitability for this job to Mr Somersby. Good-day, gentlemen.'

'Not a happy man,' Jack murmured, picking up Keeler's forgotten gun and placing it on a nearby chair before stretching out uninvited on Tom's bed. 'But what a hero!'

'Huh?'

'Well, he goes in against four desperate men stealing a payroll, drives them off with sixgun blazing, manages to wound one, and comes out without a scratch,' Jack said, and yawned mightily. 'What a hero!'

'Yeah,' said Tom, leaning against the window to watch Keeler stump angrily up towards the railyard. 'His story doesn't fit.'

'I'll say!' Jack laughed. 'When you stuck your iron under his nose and I came up behind him and put mine in his ribs, he nearly filled his pants! Is that how a hero acts?'

Blood grinned. 'There's more than that to it, though. That guy is a crook.'

'How so?'

'First, after the pay-roll being delivered personally and shown to the whole workforce, Keeler goes to sleep leaving it entirely *unguarded*? If four guys *had* come after the money, do you think they would have run off and not tried to silence the man who surprised them? Then he said that the surveyor's big pal was Ben Chaney. Do you think Boyd would be fool enough, if he was in on wrecking the railway, to be seen with another wrecker? And if he wasn't a crook he wouldn't associate with someone who was out to make trouble for the railroad with the men.'

'That makes sense,' said Jack. 'So why did Keeler lie?'

'I don't know,' said Blood, 'but lying about Chaney and Boyd puts him in on the killings of Chaney and Johnson. He probably had the idea to put their bodies in the cave. And I'll bet the old buzzard knows exactly where the money from the payroll is. One thing's in our favour, though.'

'What's that?'

'Things are moving faster for the other side than they can plan for. They're having to lie, and sloppily, so they're making mistakes.'

'On the other hand,' grinned Jack, 'it could be that they look on us as temporary, so it doesn't matter what they tell us. We're not going to live long enough to find out the truth!'

Blood grunted. 'It'll take more than I've seen so far to put me under, boy! Just the same, I think we'd do well to watch our backs extra careful from here on in, just like that old editor said. Come on, on your feet. There's work to do!'

Jack gave a mock whimper. 'Where to now? The rail-camp?'

'No,' Blood said, hitching up his gun-belt and dusting off his hat. 'I've got a feeling the enemy's a lot closer than that. There's no point going up there till I've asked a few questions here. I'm going over to talk to that editor guy, find out a few things. I want you to hang around the bar in the saloon, talk to the people, find out who they think is behind the bandits, what they think of the sheriff and so on. Listen to the scuttlebutt and buy a few drinks if needs be. Think you can do that?'

'It's a hard task,' Jack grinned, throwing a mock salute to Tom, 'but I'll do my best, sir!'

10

Blood found the offices of the *Eden Irregular Times* and Chilton's Fine Printing Ltd. down Main Street, facing the sheriff's office. The door was open and as Blood stepped inside the usual clutter and stink of a printing-shop he saw Chilton standing by a press, a sheaf of paper in his hand, arguing with a short, fat, bearded man covered in ink smudges who repeatedly pushed a pair of spectacles up his sweaty nose with the back of an inky hand.

'Damn it, Davey!' the editor said. 'If the machine's broken, then mend it. I need a special edition out as soon as possible.'

'It isna' possible,' the fat man said in a thick Scots brogue. 'You machine is nigh boogered, mon.'

'Well, unbooger it!' Crawford Chilton snapped, then turning towards his office saw Tom Blood in the doorway. 'Mr Blood! Step this way, please, sir.'

Tom followed Chilton into his office. 'Excuse the mess,' he said, waving his hand at shelves, desk-tops, chairs, even the floor, which were covered in proof copies of the *Times* and assorted samples of the printer's art. 'We're a busy little shop, and I only have that recalcitrant Scotsman you saw to help me. Can't spell to save his life, can't run a machine unsupervised, heaven knows why I keep him! Now, what can I do for you, Mr Blood?'

'It's this telegraph,' Blood told him. 'The one that spilt the beans on me coming down here to take on the gang. It was too convenient for my liking.'

The editor drew himself up slightly. 'I assure you, sir, that I received one,' he said, and indicating his cluttered desk said, 'It's in there somewhere, if you can wait a moment.'

Tom held up his hand. 'I don't doubt you,' he said. 'I'd just like to know more about how you received it.'

'Oh, I see. Well, Alton Barnes, the editor of the *San Francisco News*, is a good friend of mine. We worked on the *New York Journal* together in our youth, and when he came out here and bought the paper, as I did mine, we agreed to keep each other posted of anything newsworthy. So . . . '

Here Chilton indicated, at the far end of the office, a small table at which was installed a telegraphist's morse key. Wires ran up the wall to disappear outside.

'At first we relied on the rather slow and irregular mail service, but now that the railway has arrived I have had this wonderful device placed in my office, and I can converse direct with San Francisco. Such are the wonders of modern times, sir.'

'So Alton Barnes telegraphed this piece about the gunfight on the train to Missoula to you?' Blood asked.

'Oh, no, not on that occasion. It came in during the evening, two days ago. The office was closed, and the young telegraphist employed by the railroad brought it to me at the saloon, as sometimes happens. Barnes obviously thought it newsworthy enough to send it immediately, and not wait till my office opened the next morning. I was very grateful. I brought out a special edition, as you saw.'

Blood thought for a moment, then asked, 'Are you sure it came from Alton Barnes?'

'I haven't checked, no, but I . . .'

'Can you?' Blood asked bluntly. 'Now?'

'Do you suspect someone?' Chilton asked, smelling a story.

'Our coming here was supposed to be a secret,' Tom said. 'When that story was published in your paper the whole valley knew we were arriving. It was a very convenient way to let those who're against the railroad know about us, without the person who warned them having to show his hand.'

'I see,' said Chilton. 'Just give me

a moment.' He seated himself at the morse key and began tapping. After a couple of minutes he raised his head. 'I'm through to Alton Barnes,' he said. He tapped in for a while, then the key at his end began to chatter in reply. Crawford Chilton scribbled on a pad, then turned to Blood after tapping out a farewell to his friend in San Francisco.

'That story was not sent by my friend,' he said. 'It was not even published in his paper, but in a rival publication.'

'I knew it!' said Blood. He was quiet for a few seconds, then asked, 'How many people knew about this arrangement with your editor friend in 'Frisco?'

'Everyone who reads the paper, I should imagine,' Chilton said with a smile. He held up a copy of the paper Tom had seen out at the cave. 'I give the man a byline. Look: 'Report taken from the *San Francisco News*'.'

'Any other telegraphs in the valley

besides this and the one at the railroad?'

'No. I pay the railroad for this wire to San Francisco, and I can tell you the charge is steep. But well worth it.'

Blood decided to change tack. 'Who's likely to be behind this gang that's trying to stop the railroad?'

'Folks say Emory Hathersage,' said the editor.

'But you don't?'

'No, I don't think so,' said Chilton. 'Even though he has most to lose when the railroad goes through Paradise Valley. He hasn't the heart for a fight.'

'How come?' asked Blood.

'Three years ago sheepmen came up out of Mexico with a flock of ten thousand or more. You know what they can do to grassland.'

'I've seen it,' Blood answered grimly. 'They're worse than locusts. What happened?'

'Well,' said the editor, 'Hathersage had a son then, as well as a daughter.

101

A boy by the name of Frank. Only twenty, and wild as they came. He took a party of men from his father's ranch — they'd all been drinking to get up courage — and they went out up the valley to drive the sheepmen out. They ran the flock over a ridge, killed the lot. Then it turned into a shooting-match with the sheepmen. They were Basque Spaniards, those sheepmen, and hard as nails. All the Spaniards were killed, eventually, but not before they'd done for three of the Hathersage spread, including Frank Hathersage.'

'How did the old man take that?'

The editor spread his hands. 'He went to pieces. Frank was his darling. He's got a daughter, a real firebrand, but Frank was going to continue the Hathersage line. Emory's wife died years before, so the old man just went inside his shell, and left the ranch to Laura, his girl, to run. She's done fairly well, too, with Johnson helping. But Emory Hathersage is not the man he was.'

'So you don't think the gang's being bossed by Hathersage? What about his daughter?'

'No, she's straight. She's a wildcat, I'll warn you. She's got a big mouth and she likes her own way, but she wouldn't kill for her land.'

'Maybe Johnson was in on it?' Blood asked. 'What kind of man was he?'

'Four-square,' Crawford replied promptly. 'Honest and hard-working. You don't know the valley, but take my word, Laura Hathersage and Johnson wouldn't have been party to those kinds of evil.'

'So what's Johnson doing dead in a cave with a known bad-hat keeping him cold company, both accused of a pay-roll robbery?' Blood asked.

'It beats me, Mr Blood,' Crawford confessed. 'My best guess is that Johnson trailed Chaney to the cave and was killed by the rest of the gang because he saw too much.'

'You knew this Chaney?'

'Yes, a real low character, a drunken

rabble-rouser. The kind who'd shoot you in the back because he hadn't the guts to face a man.'

'Well,' said Blood. 'Thanks for your time and help. Guess I'll have to take a ride out to the Hathersage spread, look the place over and meet this Laura, boss-lady.'

'Oh, you can meet her sooner than that,' said Chilton, standing on tiptoe to look out of the dirty window and across Main Street. 'She's in town. I saw her ride in half an hour back. She's over in the sheriff's office.'

'Could she have heard of Johnson's death already?' Blood asked.

'No, must be something else in the wind. My newspaperman's nose is hurting me something awful, Mr Blood. What say we step across the road and I introduce you? We can find out what she wants with the sheriff at the same time.'

'I'm with you, Chilton,' Blood said.

As they crossed the main drag Chilton warned him, 'Don't say too much in front of that sheriff. I can't put my finger on it, but I don't trust the man. He gives off a bad odour. Besides,' the editor broke off to nod at the two deputies, Mort Green and Sam Collins, who were unloading the second corpse from Crawford's buggy outside the shack which served as the town mortuary, 'my revered mother always told me that you can judge a man by the company he keeps. I dare say you heard the same?'

'I never knew your mother,' Tom answered.

11

Tom and Chilton stepped into the sheriff's office to find him sitting red-faced behind his desk being berated by a young woman.

Laura Hathersage was quite a beauty, Blood allowed. Tall and blonde, she was dressed in a buckskin riding-habit. Her long hair, the colour of winter-bleached plains grass, flowed down her back, and when she turned her gaze upon him Blood was reminded of Navaho turquoise. A black Spanish sombrero decorated with silver conchoes hung from a cord behind her back and to her right wrist was attached a black leather riding-quirt.

'Sorry for the interruption, sheriff,' Chilton apologized. 'I thought that Mr Blood ought to meet Miss Hathersage, but if we're interrupting . . . '

'You're not,' Laura Hathersage said

angrily, 'since I have had my say to our dashing sheriff, who as usual is not prepared to do anything about the news I have brought. Perhaps *you* would like to hear my news, Mr Chilton?'

'Ma'am,' the editor murmured.

'Wood Linkin's farm to the north of our spread was hit last night by the gang,' Laura said. 'The bandits killed Wood, his wife and two kids, burnt the place out. Two of our boys, rounding up strays, discovered it this morning.'

'That is appalling,' Crawford said.

'Coupled with the death of poor Dan Johnson,' Laura snapped, glaring at the discomfited sheriff, 'it doesn't take a genius to see that someone is trying to make this look like the doing of my father. His only enemy in this entire valley is the railroad.'

'The bandits are hitting the railroad too, Miss Hathersage,' Tom said mildly.

'I've heard of you,' Laura Hathersage said icily, turning to look at him. 'You're one of those two hired guns they've sent in to do the railroad's bloody work. You kill to order, Mr Blood. I didn't expect you to side with justice. Good-day to you all.'

Laura Hathersage swept out of the office without a further glance in Tom's direction. Out on the boardwalk a few idlers were standing where they had been watching the deputies unload the corpses of Johnson and Chaney. Tom followed Laura outside, attempted to hold the head of her bay as she mounted, but she pulled its head round with the reins and turned on him with a glare.

'Miss Hathersage,' Tom began, 'my brief is to stop these killings and let the politicians and lawyers decide the rights and wrongs of the railroad going through here. In all honesty . . . '

'You talk of honesty?' Laura Hathersage asked, raising her voice so that the crowd could hear her. 'Honesty? You can dress up what you do in any fancy words you like, but when you come down to it, you are no better than the scum who murdered Wood

Linkin and a defenceless woman and two children last night, Tom Blood. In all honesty, now,' she asked, throwing his words back at him with a fine edge of sarcasm, 'in all honesty, haven't you killed women and children in your time?'

Blood opened his mouth to deny it, then saw in his mind's eye a scene from his days as a young man — a boy really — with the U.S. cavalry.

It was an Indian village, his first real 'battle'. He remembered later, when he had deserted and was drifting, how a 'squawman' up in Dakota, a man who had gone Indian and married a Sioux woman, had said to him bitterly, 'Strange, ain't it, how when the Injuns win it's a massacre, when the whiteman wins, it's a great battle?'

This had been a massacre all right, bloody murder . . . The blazing tepees, the running braves, shot like quail as they ran, and the captain bending in his saddle to hack at a young Indian girl with his sabre, bellowing, 'No mercy to any, women and children too. Little lice grow to be big lice!'

He had deserted the next day, sick to the stomach with what was being done in the name of 'progress', 'civilization', 'pacification'. Never worn a uniform since.

Now it had come back again to haunt him, thrown in his face like the dirty rag it was to him.

Involuntarily he had closed his eyes for a moment, and when he opened them he saw that Laura Hathersage had been looking into his face the while, and seen the truth there.

'Ma'am,' he said quietly, getting a grip on the anger he felt, 'if you were a man you would pay for that insult here and now, but it's not my way to strike a woman.'

'No,' Laura replied contemptuously, 'it's more your style to shoot me in the back, like the rest of the railroad crew you've been sent to join.'

'I think before you say any more, Miss Hathersage, you would be best advised to leave town,' Blood said, as cold as ice.

The crowd had grown as the row had intensified, and it now included Jack, who had wandered along to see where Tom was. Laura raised her voice further so that all could hear her.

'You hear that? I am ordered out of town, the town my father helped grow, make rich, by a hired pistol. If I am found dead, shot in the back, somewhere along the trail home, you are witnesses. You will know what kind of man pulled the trigger.' She was pointing at Tom Blood as she said it.

'My father gave this town life,' Laura shouted. 'Yet now the railroad has come, many of you have turned against him. You don't care that the ranchers will go to the wall, so that you can gain a few more dollars in trade from the railroad. You shrug and say 'that's progress'. Well, you will get your progress, but it will be over the dead bodies of men like Dan Johnson, and Wood Linkin, a poor dirt-farmer, and his family, people who hurt no-one. How many more have to die before . . . '

The two deputies had been standing close, listening to Laura's speech, their faces set. Now the weasel-faced Mort Green removed a cheroot he had been chewing from his mouth, spat some tobacco out and remarked in a loud voice to Sam Collins, the other deputy, 'Seems to me that Dan Johnson should have slapped her around a mite as well as screwing her. Would have taught the Hathersage whore to keep her big mouth shut.'

Laura stepped forward, her blue eyes blazing, her colour up. She flicked her right wrist up and the quirt was in her hand as she made for the sneering deputy. She was too late, however, for out of the crowd stepped Jack Storney to confront Green.

'You dirty cur!' he snapped in fine English tones, and gave the deputy a backhand blow that sent him sprawling. As Green landed on the floor he reached for his gun-belt, and Collins seemed to be minded to do likewise. Jack dropped into a gunfighter's crouch, his hand above his Colt. He had them both cold and covered. One move and they were dead men, and they knew it.

'Go for it,' Jack invited Green. 'It would give me a great deal of pleasure to drill you where you lie. You, too, Collins, if you want to make it your fight as well.'

'Hold your play!' Dawson shouted, waddling forward. 'There's no need for that. My men were just funning!'

'I don't appreciate their humour, sir,' Jack said stiffly. He turned away and gave a small bow to Laura.

'Since the man has no breeding, I apologize for him, miss,' he said. 'May I assist you to mount? Do you require an escort to your home?'

Laura allowed Jack to hold the bay's head while she mounted, then leaned down in the saddle to offer Jack her hand.

'Thank you, sir. I don't know your name. You must be new in town?' She had not connected him with Tom Blood, not realized that Jack was the second gunfighter sent by the railroad.

'Jack Storney, miss, of Storney Hall, Derbyshire, in England,' Jack replied. He had not released her hand, and was gazing into Laura's eyes with frank admiration. Laura's colour was high again, but not with anger now.

'I am Laura Hathersage, of the Circle A spread,' she replied, by way of formal introduction. 'I hope we meet again, Jack Storney.'

'I'm sure we will, Miss Hathersage,' Jack replied, and bending his head over her hand, he kissed it.

It took centuries of breeding and a certain dash to carry it off, and Jack had both.

12

Jack stood in the dirt of the road, watching Laura Hathersage ride out of town.

'What a woman!' he breathed. 'Fire and ice! Look at the way she sits that horse!'

'She has a high opinion of us, too, but you missed out on that conversation,' Blood said drily. 'Tuck your tongue in and let's go get a drink.'

'A capital idea,' Jack said, slapping Tom on the back. 'There's someone I want you to meet. He has a very interesting story to tell.'

Inside the Cattleman's Rest, all was cool and quiet. The bar was virtually empty, save for a barkeep reading yesterday's edition of the *Eden Times*, a couple of guys playing cards, and an old swamper, who was mopping the floor down so slowly it was drying between strokes. Jack ordered a couple of bourbons, then called the swamper across.

'This is the man I want you to hear,' he told Tom. 'Seth Curtis. Used to work on the Hathersage spread. Right, Seth?'

Seth nodded, and looking at the old guy, his tattered clothes, the broken veins in his ruined face, and his rheumy, bloodshot eyes, Tom saw that Seth was a serious drinker.

Seth dragged a gnarled hand across his whiskery face and looked pointedly at the drinks before the two men. He made a dry, rasping noise in his throat.

'Set up another bourbon,' Tom called to the barkeep, but Seth waved him down.

'Make it a double shot of Ol' Rooster, will ya, Mike?' Seth asked, then added apologetically, 'It's no extra, gents. It's a cheaper brand, most folks won't drink it, say it's rotgut, but I kinda got used to

116

it over the years. Cain't drink no other now.'

Mike set down a tumbler half full of a brew so rank that Tom and Jack could smell the creosote and pepper it was laced with. Seth grasped at it eagerly, shaking so much he spilt some down his shirt-front, drained the concoction noisily, then wiped his mouth with the back of his hand and gave an appreciative sigh. Jack shuddered involuntarily.

'I was about to tell Tom here that you worked on the Hathersage ranch,' Jack said.

Seth raised bleary eyes from his empty glass and looked at Tom. 'Sure did,' he said, leaning on his mop. 'Was there for twenty year, nigh on, then the ol' feller canned me. Don't blame him none, though, considerin'.'

'Considering what?' Blood asked.

The swamper set his glass down and licked his lips, looked meaningfully into its empty depths. Blood signalled for Mike to set them up again.

'Thankee, Tom,' Seth said. 'Well, I guess you know ol' Hathersage's teetotal?'

'No?' Jack responded. 'Why's that?'

'On account of his boy that was kilt. You hear about that?'

'I heard about it. What did drink have to do with it?' Blood asked.

'A lot,' Seth said, his shaking almost gone now, and colour coming to his face. 'The boy was drunk when he attacked those sheep-herders. He was always drinkin', right from when he was old enough to get into town on his own. Used to drink with Dan Johnson. They was good friends, fact Dan was with him when he was killed, only Dan could hold his licker. He was a good boy, was Frank, but the drink was his master and it did for him, yes sir.'

'What happened after Frank was killed?' Jack prompted.

'Huh? Oh, yeah! Well, the ol' man, he went plumb crazy with grief, and said he wouldn't have no more drinking on the ranch, smashed every bottle he could find, then said any man who was caught in drink on the ol' Circle A was fired straight off. Waal, I sure didn't last long after that!'

'But Dan Johnson never got canned?' Blood asked.

'No, sir,' Seth answered. 'He more or less took over an' run the ranch. He was fond of ol' man Hathersage, an' he took a lot on himself. 'Course, Laura was the real boss, an' Emory Hathersage, he just went into his shell. Left it to Laura an' Dan. Dan was sweet on Laura, too. She didn't feel for him, but he carried a torch for her all along, I guess.'

'And now he's dead,' Jack said, signalling to the barman to refill Seth's glass.

'Yep, an' he was a good guy, y'know?' Seth said. 'Straighter'n an arrow.'

'Not according to Sheriff Dawson,' Tom said. 'He thinks Johnson was killed by that surveyor, Henry Boyd. Reckons they lifted the payroll and Boyd killed Dan for it.'

Seth snorted, lifted tired old eyes to glare at Tom.

'Dan was no thief! And Henry Boyd? He wouldn't of killed Johnson. They was good friends too!'

'Kind of hard to believe, them being on different sides,' Tom said.

'OK, maybe,' the swamper said, gulping down the crazy-juice. 'Don't take my word for it. Jus' ask Chris Parker. He's got a li'l spread right up the other end of the valley. Waal, he was 'bout fifty mile away from here, three days ago, an' he happened 'cross Johnson an' Boyd. They was with that Injun, Billy Free. Chris Parker tole me hisself when he came in here the nex' day.'

'Go on,' Jack urged. 'Tell Tom what you told me.'

Seth slammed his glass down, and both men raised a finger to order his next drink. Seth tapped the side of his nose and looked sly.

'Chris tol' me this when he was drunk. Chris sees 'em an' thinks

120

they's bandits, but then recognizes Billy Free, an' hails 'em. They were mighty secretive when he asked them what they doin' up there, said they was on a huntin' trip, but Parker sees that young Henry's got his tripod an' map-rolls in leather tubes with him.'

Blood's eyebrows were raised, and Seth, who was warming with the drink, became belligerent.

'Don't believe me, huh?' he demanded. 'Waal, no-one listens to a rummy anyway, but I'll tell yer somethin'. I ain't drowned in the sauce yet, an' folks talk to drunks like me 'cos they think I'm safe, won't remember what I hear. A man has to talk sometime, 'specially when he spends long days all alone out on the range. Who better to talk to than a soak?'

'We're listening,' Jack murmured.

'Well,' Seth said, mollified. 'They asked Chris special not to tell that he saw 'em, but he told me. An' you know what I think?' He leaned closer confidentially, and Blood and

Jack leaned backwards, near gagging at the smell of unwashed body and Ol' Rooster. Seth didn't notice, confided in a triumphant tone, 'I think they weren't huntin' at all.'

'What were they doing, Seth?' Blood asked.

'Whatever they doin' it was mixed up with the railroad,' Seth said, nodding his grey head wisely. ' 'Cos I saw Dan Johnson yesterday evenin', when he got back from his trip with Billy Free an' Henry Boyd. Dan come in here alone, an' with bein' away from the bottle for three days, he pitched into it a mite. Then he told me somethin'.' Here the swamper paused and looked again into his glass. It was quickly filled.

'Thanks, gents,' Seth said. He made for the glass, but Jack held the old man's skinny arm gently.

'Tell us what you heard,' he said.

'Oh, yeah. Well, Dan Johnson stood right here, early las' night an' he said to me, 'Seth,' he said, 'mebbe folks is in a stew 'bout nothin' over this railroad. I wouldn't be surprised,' he says to me, 'if'n the railroad don't go through this valley at all,' an' he's chucklin' like he's real pleased 'bout somethin'. 'Seth,' he tells me, 'if I was a rich man, I'd buy stocks in that northern line that's goin' through.' That's what he tol' me. By that time, o'course, he was pretty drunk, but I got the opinion he wasn't jus' blowin' hot air out his rear. He tol' me that after tonight, the railroad was goin' to end in Eden.'

'Did he tell anyone else?' Blood asked.

'No, sir. He come in early, got pretty drunk, an' left early. Only really talked to me, 'cos I was hittin' on him for a few drinks.' Seth looked into his empty glass, said meaningfully, 'He was a generous guy, was Dan.' His glass was filled once more.

'So he rode out to the Hathersage spread?' Jack asked.

'Oh, no!' Seth said. 'He daresn't do that. He was drunk. Ol' man Hathersage might have seen him, an' he would have been skinned alive for bein' drunk. He went to the widow-woman's place.'

'Who's she?' Blood asked idly.

'Amy Croft. She's Bob Croft's, the last sheriff's widow. Got a little place just outside o'town, on the road up the valley. Sells milk an' eggs in town, few chickens, greens an' such stuff. Makes a livin'. She an' Dan had what you might call an understandin' for the last year or so, since Dan kinda give up on Laura. Amy's still young an' got her looks. Folks thought they might marry soon. Anyway, Dan said he was goin' there, sleep it off, an' that's the last I saw of him.'

The batwings flew back and the swamper looked around, dropped his eyes and began mopping the floor around Tom's and Jack's feet.

'I've said too much,' he whispered. 'Thanks for the drinks, you guys. Don't tell where you heard the stuff I told yer, huh?'

Blood looked round. In the doorway

stood Sheriff Dawson, flanked by his deputies. They were glaring over at him as if he had pissed in their father's beer. Blood gave them a thin smile and tipped his hat to them, while Jack pretended to turn his back, watching the three through the corner of his eye, in case they fanned out, when he just might take a walk to the other corner of the bar, loosen his gun the while, lessen the odds a mite.

The sheriff kept walking till he fetched up against the bar, where he stuck his thumbs in his belt and tried to look hard. He fooled no-one.

'I don't appreciate what yer sidekick just done with my deppities,' he told Blood.

'What's that?' Blood asked, taking the excuse of rolling a smoke to look down, not showing Dawson his face.

'They made my boys look small in a town they got to control,' Dawson replied, while Green and Collins continued to look poison at Jack.

'That's down to them,' Blood replied, smoothing off his smoke and wetting the gummed edge. 'They insulted the lady.'

'Waal,' Dawson blustered, his squint eye wandering alarmingly, 'I'm only goin' to tell yer once. I don't want you and this trigger-happy punk hangin' around town too much . . . '

'By God, but you've a cool cheek,' Jack interrupted. 'Punk, is it?' His colour was up and he was itching for a fight.

'You got the drop on me back there, pistolero,' Green sneered, speaking round a well-chewed cheroot. Maybe he imagined that it made him look tough. 'But a hired gun's just another way of sayin' bandit, an' when this gang's settled, I'm gonna come lookin' for you!'

The last few words Green spoke were somewhat choked off, since he found that Jack had very smoothly brought a .45 up into an area directly below his epiglottis, and was pressing quite insistently with the muzzle against the deputy's flesh. His cheroot flew from his lips and his eyes opened wide in alarm.

'After your insult that is to be taken as a promise,' Jack hissed, his face white. 'No, sheriff, don't touch your gun, or I'll blow your boy away and then plug your fat carcase too! Now, Mort Green, to resume our conversation. I've caught you twice before, and this makes three; so, as they say, the third time pays for all. Why not step outside and settle directly? I'm tired of hearing you talk big and deliver small.'

'Easy, Jack,' Blood said, stepping up to Jack, but taking care not to step into the line of fire. 'We've got a job to do and can't afford to be distracted. Dawson, tell your boys to cool down.'

'OK you guys, back off,' Dawson grated. 'We ain't doin' any good tryin' to kill each other.'

Jack holstered his gun and stepped

back, keeping a wary eye on Green, who rubbed his throat and looked sullen.

'Now,' Blood said, leaning back against the bar and blowing smoke up to the ceiling, 'let's get a few things straight, Dawson. You may be the law in Eden, putting drunks in the tank, collecting taxes and such, but where the railroad's concerned, me and Jack's the law. What we say goes, and you try and get in the way, like you've done twice already, and you're going to get hurt. Savvy?'

The sheriff looked poison, then said lamely, 'All I'm telling you to do is get out there and catch the gang, 'stead of hanging round the saloons listenin' to some old lush's scuttlebutt.'

'In my own time,' Blood said. 'There's a lot of country out there. I don't intend to go playing Catch Me Kate all over the valley and up in the mountains on your say-so. 'Course, if you've any gripes, get on to the president, see what he says. I hear tell he's a personal friend of yours.'

'Huh?' Dawson said, looking mystified.

'That is just what I have done,' interrupted Warren Keeler from over the batwings, where he had been listening in. He stepped into the saloon and handed Tom a yellow telegraph-form. 'It came directly from Hasland J. Coldwell ten minutes ago,' he said smugly. 'As you will see, he agrees with me on your next course of action.'

The telegraph read 'Whilst confirming your free hand in this investigation, must agree with Keeler stop Hathersage instigator of all trouble in valley stop Believe ranch to be gang headquarters stop Check place out first. Regards Coldwell.'

'Any reply?' Keeler enquired with a triumphant smile.

'No,' Blood said calmly. 'We'll ride out there first thing tomorrow. Better turn in now. It's been a long day. Gentlemen.'

'Oh, Blood,' Keeler called. He walked

over and said softly, 'While you're out at the ranch, look out for a palomino, very fine-marked. Two people who've encountered the gang say the leader of the gang was riding such an animal.'

Blood tipped his hat and made for the stairs. Not till Tom was at the head of the stairs leading to his room and was looking back down did Jack take his eyes off Dawson and the others and make his own way up to the first floor.

'What the hell got into Dawson and his boys back there?' Jack asked Tom who had been covering his back also. 'They damned near started a gunfight.'

'I get the feeling that they don't like us hanging around town asking questions,' Blood said. 'They'd prefer us out in the country, where an accident can be arranged. We're finding out too much, they're getting rattled.'

They looked down on the bar. The barkeep was talking sternly to Seth, telling the old swamper he couldn't have any credit, that if he gave him any more drink he'd go on a spree and not work for days, that he already owed two months wages and besides . . . At the other end of the bar Warren Keeler was in a huddle with the deputies, the group casting occasional glances in their direction.

'They're starting to show their hands,' Blood murmured, then to Jack, 'You're too rash for this game, Jack. Take it easy. You let the deputy get you angry, and an angry man is a careless one. Careless spells dead around here.'

'You're right, Tom. You were dragged in too. I apologize,' Jack said. 'Well it's me for bed, to dream of seeing the divine Laura Hathersage tomorrow!'

'Yeah,' Blood mused. 'Let's call in on the widow-woman, Amy Croft, on our way out to the Circle A. See what she can tell us about Johnson's little secret. I'd like to know just why the railroad's going to end in Eden. 'Night, Jack. Keep your door locked and your pistol handy.'

13

By the time that Sheriff Dawson and the two deputies found Seth Curtis he was so desperate for a drink that he would have followed the devil down into hell for a shot of rotgut. There were only two saloons in town. He was banned from one and his credit was cut off at the Cattleman's. No-one in town would stand him a drink. What was he to do?

They ran him to earth in his lean-to shack, back of the livery stables, feverishly searching the collection of old rags he looked upon as his spare duds. Maybe, just maybe, there was a coin he'd overlooked in one of the pockets. It had happened before. Just get enough for a drink and maybe someone would stand him another one or two. Maybe, maybe. He muttered and swore as he searched, crouching on his haunches, and was impervious to the slight noise of the three men as they entered the shack. It was only when he turned to see what was blocking the light from the guttering candle on the packing-case by the side of his reeking bed that he saw them, looking down and smiling at him.

'Evenin', Seth,' Dawson said in a mock-friendly tone. 'Hope it ain't too late an hour to come callin'?'

'Why, I'm sure Seth don't mind,' Green said, pausing to light another of his foul-smelling cheroots at the candle. ' 'Specially when he sees what you brung him, Jake.'

Sam Collins sniggered, and Dawson shot him a warning look. 'Give Seth his present, Mort,' he said smoothly. 'There y'go, Seth. Happy days, old-timer.'

Mort held out a full bottle of whiskey. It caught the light in its amber depths and held Seth like a snake fixing a monkey.

'Drink up,' Mort invited, uncorking

the bottle and putting it into Seth's grasp.

'What . . . '

'We just want a little talk,' Jake Dawson said. 'Thought it'd be more sociable over a snort of whiskey. Drink!'

The last word was snapped out, and Seth took a good long slug. He offered the bottle round, but it was refused and again he was urged to drink. Soon he was halfway down the bottle and feeling its glow spread through him.

'OK, Seth. We done somethin' for you,' Dawson said, standing over the swamper. 'Now you do somethin' for us, huh?'

'What you want doin'?' Seth quavered. The trio didn't look too friendly, even though they were still smiling down at him. He made to rise, but Collins pushed him back down again.

'We don't want nothin' doin',' Dawson assured him. 'We're just curious, ain't that right, boys?'

The 'boys' nodded their assent, and Dawson urged Seth to drink some more. Seth refused, and Collins took the bottle and fed it to Seth, holding him roughly by the back of the neck, so that he cried out. Some of the whiskey ran out of his mouth and down his chin.

'All we want to know is what you were tellin' Tom Blood and his English sidekick,' Dawson said.

'Oh, nothin' much,' Seth said lamely.

'Nothin'?' Dawson asked. 'Seems to me that you were pretty thick with him when we walked in, eh, boys?'

'Jake, I think it might save us all some time if I was to talk to Seth,' Green said. 'I think I can make him see reason.'

Dawson nodded his assent, and after Seth had been made to take another pull at the whiskey bottle Mort came to stand close in front of Seth. He nodded to Collins, standing behind the swamper, and the stocky little deputy reached down and twisted the swamper's arms back so that Seth threw his head up with the pain. Mort Green blew on his cheroot till it was cherry-red.

'Now the thing is, Seth,' he crooned, bringing the cheroot's burning tip closer and closer to the old man's face, 'Jake brung you a bottle of whiskey an' you're being downright unsociable. Do you get my . . . point!'

Seth got the point all right, and Mort laughed sadistically as he drove it into the old man's right cheek. Seth screamed a mite, and Collins gripped his neck and slapped a hand over the swamper's mouth. Mort touched the cheroot to Seth's cheek again.

When he was released from Collins' grip and Mort had stepped back the pain, the fear, and the tongue-loosening whiskey made Seth eager to talk. He told them everything, spilling the words out quickly so that they were almost slurred.

'My, my,' Dawson murmured when Seth had finished. 'What a tale our cat's got, as my old grannie used to say.'

'Can I go now, fellers?' Seth pleaded, trying to get to his feet. Collins kicked him hard in the back and he went sprawling at Dawson's feet. The sheriff squatted down and smiled into Seth's frightened, tortured face.

'Now, you sure you not forgot anything?' he asked, and once more Mort Green came close, puffing on his cheroot to get it fired up.

'No, no, honest I ain't,' Seth sobbed. 'I told you everything, Jake.'

'Yeah,' agreed Dawson, 'I reckon you have, Seth. I reckon you told us too much, in fact. What *can* we do about that, boys?'

Collins snuffled out a nasty laugh. Mort just chewed on his cheroot.

'I could stay here and tuck him into bed for a good, long sleep,' he suggested.

'No, no,' Dawson said. He reached down and gripped Seth's collar, hauled him to his feet and stared almost lovingly into the drunken man's terrified face. He pretended to sniff the air.

'Seth Curtis, you been drinkin'!' he said in mock horror. 'He's drunk, fellers!'

'Oh, mercy me!' Mort said, his hand to his mouth. Dawson back-handed Seth across the face, then threw him across to the deputies, who gripped his arms between them. The sheriff retrieved the whiskey bottle from the floor and stuck it in Seth's jacket pocket.

'Now, I think you need to walk it off a while,' Dawson said to him, stepping to the door and looking out into the deserted alley. 'Oh, and boys? I think he'd better take some water with his next drink. Let's go, Seth.'

14

It was early morning, the town hardly stirring, when Blood and Jack rode out of town and took the eastern trail that wound the twenty or so miles to the Hathersage spread. For about a mile it followed the railroad track, and their horses were unsettled when a locomotive pulling a flatbed laden with rails and ties steamed past and set its whistle shrieking, but soon the track veered away to bridge the distant river, and they settled into a steady trot, eating up the miles. In the distance, some five miles out of town, they could see the widow Croft's farm by the side of the trail.

It was a neat, well-ordered farm they saw, when they reached its few fields. Green stuff and Indian corn for sale to the townsfolk, with a few dairy cows grazing on a slope, while close to the two-storey wooden house were pig-sties and hen-runs, and a large, red-painted barn.

'One woman runs all this?' Tom asked in wonder.

'She had Johnson helping her,' Jack said. 'Remember?'

'Even so,' Tom said, looking around, then nodding to a field that had recently been ploughed he said, 'Notice the soil?' It was red, the same colour as that found on Dan Johnson's boots when they had examined him in the cave.

Just then a slim, dark-haired woman in her early thirties wearing a long black dress and clean white apron, came out of the barn. Just far enough for the two riders to see that she held close to her hip a shotgun. At the moment it was pointing to the earth, but she kept her distance and called to them, asking what their business was. Tom dismounted carefully, and with his hands held well away from his gunbelt, introduced himself and Jack.

'You can walk up,' the woman said,

and Jack dismounted too and together they walked their horses into the yard and tied them to a rail in the shade of the barn. A large mastiff, chained close by the barn door, blocking entrance to the barn, growled low in its throat and then lunged forward at Jack.

'Easy, Fury,' the woman called in a low, pleasant voice. 'Will you step inside the house please, gentlemen?'

Close to, they could see that she was an attractive woman, even though she was simply dressed for her work around the house and her chestnut-coloured hair had been hastily pinned up. Her eyes were a light green, and though she wouldn't see thirty again, Jack thought, as she handed him a cup of coffee, her complexion was clear and smooth. Her figure was full and very feminine too, he thought, as he watched her brush her apron down, smooth it out, then walk around the table to Tom with his tin mug. Tom saw the hard, work-calloused hands, and the sadness in her eyes also. This was a woman who was suffering, but bearing it with dignity.

'Well, gentlemen, how can I help you?' Amy Croft asked, seating herself at the table so that she could see both men.

'It's about Dan Johnson, ma'am,' Tom said, uncomfortable as ever when in the company of women. 'We understand that you and he were, well, we were told in town . . . '

The widow did not take her eyes off Tom's face as he stumbled to find words to express what he wanted to say, to discover just where Dan Johnson had been staying on his last night on earth.

Calmly she said, 'We were lovers, Mr Blood. Does that answer your question?'

'Yes, ma'am. Did you see him the night before last?'

'Yes, I did. He came to stay the night with me. He often stayed. You see, since my husband died . . . '

'Mrs Croft,' Blood said, 'you have no need to explain your friendship to us.

We just want to find out about Dan's killing.'

'I have nothing to be ashamed of, and I would like you to know,' Amy said, looking at Tom. 'Since my husband was murdered, I have had to take on occasional help on the farm. Dan was a friend of my husband's. He came and helped too, and we reached what you would call 'an understanding'. We were both very lonely, both of us had lost someone we loved, and I hoped that in time Dan would marry me. That did not happen.'

She busied herself, fetching the coffee-pot from the stove and refilling their mugs.

'Please don't distress yourself, Mrs Croft,' Jack said as she turned away, but she ignored him and poured Tom's coffee.

'But you want to know about last night?' she said, seating herself at the table and fixing a stray wisp of hair which had come undone.

'Did Dan Johnson come here?' Blood asked.

She nodded. 'Yes. He came. He had been drinking, which was unusual for him. I think he still had the occasional drinking-session in town, but in the main he had stopped. He knew that I did not like men who drank, and his employer, Mr Hathersage, is totally against it. However, he carried his drink well, and I did not at first realize how drunk he was, though I could smell whiskey on him.'

'What gave him away?'

Amy Croft looked away a moment, reliving the night. 'I invited him to stay the night, and we were in my room. I was pleased to see him, as he had not been over for a few days. I asked him where he had been, and he said he had been on a hunting-trip with some buddies. Then he said . . . ' she broke off, bit her lip, and her eyes moistened. Jack was about to speak, but Blood gave him a warning look. Soon she looked back into Blood's face and spoke calmly.

'He told me that our liaison must end, that he would not come here again. He said that he had discovered something which would save the valley from the railroad, and that he thought when it became known, that the young lady whom he truly loved . . . '

Again she stopped, fighting her tears.

'Would that be Miss Laura Hathersage?' Tom enquired gently.

'You know about her?' Amy asked. She lifted a corner of her apron and dried her eyes. 'Excuse me, gentlemen. Yes. He thought that if he saved the valley then Laura would look more favourably on him, might consent to marry him. You see, most men would have asked the other woman first, then broken off our relationship, but Dan was a very honest man. He liked to do the honourable thing. So he told me that he was going to propose to Laura Hathersage again, that he thought this time she would accept him.'

'What happened then?'

'I lost my temper. I told him he was a fool, and to get out. I told him he could not stay in my bed and think of another woman the while.'

'Did he go?' Blood asked.

Amy Croft nodded. 'He went. It was late, I do not know the exact time. I was too . . . distressed.'

'Could he have ridden over to the rail-camp and taken the pay-roll, do you think?' Jack asked.

'No,' she said emphatically. 'Dan could be reckless at times, but he was a very straight man, that's why I loved him. And by the time he left, the whiskey he had drunk was having a definite effect on him. He must have been drinking while he rode up here; had a bottle in his saddlebags, I think. I watched him go, and he had difficulty mounting his horse. He was weaving in the saddle when he rode away. I almost called him back, told him he could stay the night in another room, but too much had been said by then.'

Blood nodded understandingly, and

let the silence in the room grow while he drank his coffee.

'I need to know about your husband also, Mrs Croft,' he said eventually.

'What of him?' the widow enquired, looking at Tom directly.

'I understand that he was killed too, and his killers were never caught?'

'The railroad had him killed, Mr Blood,' Amy Croft said. 'There is no doubt in my mind about that.'

'What makes you so sure, if you don't mind my asking?'

'When the railroad was just mooted, and their agents were sniffing around, two men came out to the farm to talk to my husband. I saw them from a distance. He spoke to them out in the fields, and very soon sent them packing.'

'Do you know who they were?'

'One of them was Keeler, the chief engineer for the contractors who are building the railroad. I had not seen him before, but I recognized him some months later when he came to the

147

valley with the railroad. The other man I didn't know and haven't seen since.'

'What did he look like?' Blood asked.

Amy Croft considered for a while. 'He was younger,' she said slowly. 'He was tall, slim, quite good-looking, I'd say. Dark hair. Guarded in his speech.'

'What do you mean, guarded, Mrs Croft? I thought you were at a distance from them?'

'I mean that he was careful. He looked around him before talking. He held his mouth in a strange way when he spoke, too.'

'What did they want? Did your husband tell you?'

'No. I asked, but he was too angry to talk much. He just said that it was business, but there were some things a man would not do. I got the impression they had tried to buy him, make him the railroad's man. He went back to work in the fields. Two days later he was found shot outside the town, and I say the railroad killed him, damn them to hell.'

There was no more to be said. Blood reached for his hat where it lay under his chair, then rose to his feet.

'I want to thank you, Mrs Croft,' he said, 'for being so frank with us.'

'Not at all,' she replied calmly. 'I hope it helps. I hear you are very good at your job, Mr Blood, and I would like to see Bob's and Dan's killers found and gunned down. Either that or dancing on the end of a rope. Is that wrong of me, do you think?'

'No, ma'am, quite natural,' Blood assured her. He had been up against many killers, put them away without compunction, and had no worries on that score. Many could talk of killing for vengeance. Few who talked so hotly and bravely about revenge could pull the trigger or place the noose round the murderer's neck if it ever came to it. Looking into the widow's steady eyes, seeing the determined jut to her chin, Blood knew that here was one who had courage to go with her conviction, and he found a deeper respect for her.

'I have one great regret, something that I have to live with,' Amy Croft said, as she walked with them to their horses.

'What's that, ma'am?' Jack asked.

'I sent Dan out to his death that night. If he had stayed with me, his killers would not have found him.'

'You could have acted no other way, and if you'll excuse my boldness,' Jack said, 'I believe that Dan Johnson did not know what a treasure he threw away when he turned his back on you.'

The widow looked into Jack's face, her eyes moist.

'Thank you, sir,' she whispered.

As they passed through the gate Blood leaned down to the widow, where she stood holding the gate open.

'One last question,' he said. 'Did you hear any shooting after Dan left here?'

'No,' Amy Croft replied, 'but then I

wouldn't, would I?'

'Why not?' Blood asked.

'Do you not know?' she asked with a sad smile. 'Did no-one tell you when they were telling you all the gossip about my shamelessness, about my husband and my lover? I am almost totally deaf, Mr Blood. When people wish to talk to me, I must follow their lips.'

15

A couple of miles further on they found where Dan Johnson had been killed. Blood had been watching both sides of the red dirt trail intently, and where the road took a small rise he pulled back on his reins and pointed to a place at the side of the road where the weeds and bushes had been broken down. The two dismounted to take a close look.

The side of the road dipped sharply and down a steep slope could be seen a trail through the herbage where something heavy had smashed its way to the bottom. Flies and the sweet smell of death rose up to meet them as they made their way down, causing Jack, who was in front, almost to gag. He turned to Tom.

'There's a dead horse down here. Looks like its neck was broken in the fall. It's been covered over with branches and stuff.'

Tom pointed to another spot where a smaller track had been broken through the undergrowth.

'Seems to me that Johnson was shot up there on the road. The horse bolted or shied, came down here and just over there Johnson fell off, rolled down the bank till he landed in this spot. The horse went on to the bottom, broke its neck in the fall. Then you can see where the killers — there's more than one set of bootprints here — grabbed a hold of Johnson's body between them and dragged him back up, which is how he got those scuff-marks on his boots, and the red soil inside them.'

'So he didn't take the pay-roll?'

'No.'

'Bushwhacked,' Jack said grimly.

'Yeah, that's about the size of it,' Tom answered. 'Now, whose speciality would that be?'

★ ★ ★

Coincidentally, the guys Tom and Jack were both thinking of were at that moment discussing them.

' . . . Widow Croft, Billy Free, that surveyor, and Blood and his sidekick,' said Collins, numbering them off on his fingers, then adding up slowly. 'That's five. Hell-fire, that's a lot of killin' we got to do!'

Dawson leant back in his chair and pushed the whiskey bottle across his office desk to the two deputies, who poured slugs of it into their coffee.

'Don't worry none about Blood and Storney,' he said. 'Keeler's fixed a little surprise for them this morning at Hathersage's ranch. They won't be coming back alive. As for that Boyd feller, hell, he's probably dead already. Keeler's damned sure he got a shot into him when he was escapin'.'

'So why ain't we found the body?' Mort Green demanded. 'We searched everywhere he could of got to.'

' 'Cos he's with Billy Free. We trailed Boyd's blood-tracks by daylight next day as far as we could, didn't we? And where'd they end?'

'In a whole mess of moccasin marks, then off onto solid rock, and away into the mountains,' Green answered.

'Right, which means he's with the Injun, who's responsible for taking him and Johnson up the valley in the first place and showing them what's lying ahead of the railroad. No, that surveyor's dead, mark my words. Keeler says he got him spang in the middle of his skinny back, an' from the amount of blood he lost, I'd say he was done for. Five'll get y'ten the Injun's hid the body, an' hightailed it. We'll not see his yeller hide again.'

'So that only leaves the widow-woman to keep from talking,' said Collins. 'How do we know that Johnson told her anything? He didn't tell old Seth the full story.'

'We don't know,' said Dawson shortly. 'But Keeler said we had to play safe. All the same, I don't like it when women are involved.'

'Suits me,' said Mort Green, chewing on an unlit cheroot. 'Easier to kill.' Then he smacked his thigh. 'Got it!'

'What?' the sheriff asked.

'Why, how to kill three birds with one stone! Look, we kill the widow Croft tonight, leave mocassin-prints, maybe a bit of beadwork or Injun clothing around the house, make it look like Free killed her — he hangs around there sometimes, don't he?'

'Yeah,' said Jack slowly. 'She used to pay him to work the farm for her.'

'Right. If we make everyone think Free's killed a white woman, we get the whole damn territory looking for him. He'll soon be caught, and that'll lead us to Boyd, if he's still alive. Who knows, the guys that catch Free'll probably be so angry they'll string him up there and then, save us a job! He won't have time to talk; 'sides, who's going to believe a murdering Injun?'

'Yeah,' said Dawson. 'Yeah. It might just work at that . . .'

16

The Circle A stood at the north-western edge of the valley. It faced the trail, which wound round the foot of a steep-shelving slope a half-mile away, at the base of which was a jumble of fallen rocks and scree. Beyond, the valley side was sheer, but further along the hills became more gentle and climbed up towards the steeper ranges of the Steins Mountains, inhabited by the Apache, their safe route in and out of nearby Mexico for centuries.

Blood and Jack reined in and looked at the ranch. There were cattle in the pens, a windmill turned lazily, and a dozen or so men could be seen moving around the outbuildings. The ranch-house itself was a long, low hacienda, in front of which a large man sat in a rocking-chair, working at some leather harnesses over his knees. Hens picked around his feet and a yellow dog slept by his side, curled nose to tail.

'A pleasant spot, eh?' Jack drawled. 'Are we safe, d'you think?'

'We'll see,' said Blood, spurring his horse on. 'Listen, when I get talking to Hathersage, you have a casual walk around the place. Keeler said the boss of the gang rides a really smart palomino. Take a look in the stables if you can. And talk to the ranch-hands, listen for Southern accents.'

As they rode up to the hacienda the big man in the chair got up, laid down the harness and walked to meet them. He was tall, well over six feet, though his shoulders were slumped and he seemed to slouch tiredly as he walked out. Blood saw a man of sixty or so with a full head of grey hair, handsome once, but the flesh of his face was pouchy, suggesting that he had ceased to exercise. Looking into the dull eyes, Tom saw a man had given up on life.

'Howdy,' the man greeted them. 'I'm

Emory Hathersage. You'll be Tom Blood?'

'News travels fast around here,' Blood said, extending his hand. 'My colleague, Jack Storney.'

Emory gave a bleak smile. 'My daughter described you, Mr Blood. She said you would be out this way soon. I must apologize for her discourtesy yesterday. She's a firebrand, I know. She's not around at the moment, which is perhaps best. Would you care to step inside, gentlemen, take some refreshment?'

Blood accepted, but Jack refused and Emory invited him to take a look around the ranch, almost as if he had expected the two to search it for any evidence of the gang's presence.

'Come this way, Mr Blood,' Hathersage said courteously, waving him down a long covered way around the side of the hacienda. Indian corn and peppers were laid out to dry in the central courtyard, and an old Indian woman was weaving in one corner. Hathersage called to her in Spanish and she laughed, rose and went through a doorway.

'That's my late wife's maid, Maria,' Hathersage said. 'Now she cares for me in my old age.'

Blood wanted to tell the man he'd seen older. That he'd seen guys with ten years or more on him prong a bronco twenty miles through hail and mud to dance at a wedding or watch a prizefight, but then he shrugged to himself as they walked on. It wasn't his business if the guy wanted to give up and die of self-pity.

'So, Mr Blood, just what does a railroad detective like yourself do — apart from kill people who get in your way?' Hathersage asked, seating himself in a leather-covered armchair, and waving Blood to another. The dog had followed him in, and he was stroking its ears absent-mindedly.

Tom blinked. The old guy still had some pepper left! He'd sneaked up on him with that one! He cleared his throat to answer, and at that moment

Maria shuffled in with a tray on which rested several small pitchers, glasses, and plates of cold meats and corn biscuits.

'Allow me to pour you a drink,' Hathersage offered. 'We have lime-juice, lemon or orange. There's no alcohol on this ranch, I'm pleased to say.'

My ass, Blood thought. With my nose for men's ways, I could walk out of here and find my particular poison in less time than it takes Maria to squeeze those drinks. As many men you got working on this ranch means as many — or more — bottles hid up somewhere.

'As it comes,' Blood said, taking a token glass, not drinking. 'You ask about my job as a railroad detective? I'm not denying I've killed some guys in my time, Mr Hathersage.'

'That's as well,' Emory murmured. He reached down and held up a copy of the *Eden Irregular Times* with its screaming banner that labelled Tom a killer. 'As you said, news travels fast.'

'I'm more than a hired gun,' Tom said quietly. 'I'm the law where there is no law. I'm the man who goes where the scum breeds and grows bold. I find out what's true, and I punish what is evil, and if I kill what's in my way, then so be it. I happen to be proud of what I sometimes have to do, Mr Hathersage. Lesser men may sneer, but they don't have the balls to do what I do.'

'Good for you,' Hathersage said. 'I like a man who defends himself. But you see, we all think we're making America grow, Tom Blood.' He stood and walked to the far wall, where glass had been placed instead of brick. 'Come see here.'

Tom stood by Hathersage's side and looked far up the valley.

'This valley hasn't changed since I first rode in forty years ago with three hundred head, and my wife herding the beef alongside of me.' Blood made to speak, but the rancher waved him down. 'OK, so change has to come, but if the railroad drives right up the valley and out the other end, it'll tear the heart out of it. The railroad'll get prime land-grants, sell 'em piecemeal, and all you see now will be grubbed up by small farms. I can't let that happen, because what I'm looking at now, the Paradise I settled and lived in with my woman, that's America too.'

'So what are you going to do?' Blood asked him quietly. 'The railroad's here. You don't legally own all this, and the railroad's got the law on its side.'

'I've still got some political clout,' Hathersage said fiercely. 'I have friends in Washington who . . . '

He broke off as Jack walked into the room, his hands held high. Behind him, holding a cocked Colt Peacemaker in his back, walked Laura Hathersage, dressed in riding-breeches. Jack smiled at Blood and gave a small shrug.

'We just bumped into each other,' he told Tom, with a small backward jerk of his head to Laura.

'What in thunder are you doing,

Laura?' Hathersage demanded angrily.

'I caught this character in the stables,' Laura snapped.

'I tried to explain that I had permission,' Jack said, still with the gun trained on him.

'That's right,' Hathersage said, 'I told Mr Storney to take a look around. We have nothing to hide here on the Circle A.'

'Did that include telling him he could search Sage's saddlebags?' Laura asked, giving Jack a prod with the gun's barrel. 'Because that was what he was doing when I caught him, going through them like a thief.'

Hathersage turned to Tom Blood. 'Your colleague has abused my hospitality,' he said quietly. 'I think you had better leave.' He signalled to Laura and she lowered her gun, let Jack pass with Tom.

At the door to the hacienda, as they untied their mounts, Emory Hathersage said simply, 'You are not welcome on my ranch in future.'

'Stick to the trail if you ride this way again,' Laura said, the Colt still in her hand. 'Stay off our land.'

'Until this gang's caught, Miss Hathersage, I intend to ride where I will, and no man — or woman in breeches — will keep me off open range,' Blood said quietly, gathering up his reins and turning the horse's head. He tipped his hat to them. 'Good-day, Mr Hathersage, ma'am.'

★ ★ ★

Up amongst the rocks a scrawny little guy squinted down the sights of a Sharps .70 buffalo rifle. He lay on his back, his legs crossed, and he kept the long barrel steadied by resting it between the vee of his boots.

The Sharps, also known by the buffalo-hunters as a 'business rifle' was a precision killing-instrument. Noted for its range and accuracy it was lethal at over a mile, and in the hands of an expert like Nate it could be placed in

165

the centre of a dollar-piece at half the distance. In the sights, Blood's upper torso showed clearly.

'Easy, easy,' Nate breathed, watching the small figures riding towards him, then to the man behind him he said, 'which 'un d'ye want me to drap first, Fletcher? Blood or his boy?'

The big, heavy man squeezed in alongside the sharpshooter, kept his spyglass steady, held to his left eye, since the right was missing, covered by a leather eyepatch which served only to draw attention to the huge scar that bisected his face. Finally he grunted and rolled over from where he had been lying, belly down, to a sitting position.

'One on the left's Blood,' he said, idly scratching the scar. 'Kill him first, Nate, then drop t'other if'n you've time.'

'Oh, they's time,' Nate assured the gang-leader. 'They's no cover for quarter a mile either way. I kin reload this li'l beauty an' still have time to shift the sights to where the other runs to.'

Nate inserted a cartridge and pushed up the trigger-guard which served as the under-lever. Another swift check through the sights, and he was in the act of curling his finger round the rear of the two triggers, the 'set' hair-trigger, when Fletcher, who had been looking through his spyglass toward the ranch, said, 'What the . . . ? Hold yer fire, Nate!'

'Huh?' Nate turned, frowning.

'Take a look-see at ol' Hathersage an' his girl through the glass.' Fletcher proffered the spyglass to Nate and pointed down to the ranch. 'I plump missed it 'afore. Whit d'y'see in the Hathersage female's hand?'

Grudgingly Nate took the glass from Fletcher's hand and looked through it. 'A pistol,' he said. 'She's holding a pistol. Now kin I shoot?'

'Don't be in sech a blamed hurry,' Fletcher said slowly. 'Now why should she be holding a pistol?'

'Keeler said Laura Hathersage had a spat with Blood in Eden when they met,' said Nate. 'Looks like she's done ordered him off the ranch at gunpoint.'

'That's right,' Fletcher replied, rasping his hand over his chin thoughtfully. 'Keeler said Dawson was there, told him that she was shouting off to folk that Blood had threatened her life. Now, try an foller' this: what happens if we kill Blood?'

Nate furrowed his brow. Thinking wasn't his strong point. 'Folks'll say that Hathersage ordered the killing when Blood came to the ranch. Can I shoot him now? Ain't much time left to get 'em both, Fletcher.'

'No,' said the leader. 'An' mebbe the railroad'll send down more men, an' a war will break out. An' mebbe not. But what happens if we wait till Laura Hathersage takes her afternoon ride an' shoot *her*?'

'By God!' Nate said, brightening at the prospect of using the Sharps eventually. 'Ever'one'll think that Blood

and his sidekick got her, after orderin'
her out o' town, threatenin' her life,
an' then bein' run off the ranch
themselves.'

'Exackly,' Fletcher nodded. 'Kill
her, an' the whole valley will go
up. Ranchers and farmers agin the
railroad. It'll be a bloodbath!'

'But . . . ' Nate looked wistfully at
Blood and Storney, riding up below
them, heading for the trail to Eden,
'ain't we gonna shoot these jaspers too?
Keeler said we had to.'

'Keeler ain't my boss!' Fletcher
snapped. ' 'Sides, he ain't here, an'
this is too good an oppertoonity ter
miss! Hello, where're *they* goin'?'

Fletcher carefully leaned out over the
rock to watch Blood and Storney, who,
once out of sight of the ranch, had
dismounted and were walking back,
leading their horses behind the rocks
some forty feet or so below Nate and
Fletcher to watch the ranch.

'They spyin' on the ranch!' whispered
Nate. The two railroad detectives

disappeared from sight below.

'Perfect!' breathed Fletcher. 'That means that when we shoot the Hathersage bitch we hightail it out of here, an' leave them two to take the rap! Nate, go tell the boys up top to keep quiet and be ready for a quick getaway when they hear your cannon!'

Nate nodded and stealthily crept up a gully to where the rest of the gang were waiting with the horses. Fletcher pulled a gold pocket-watch out and looked at it. Another hour or so till she took her afternoon ride, and then . . . He grinned to himself and settled down to wait.

17

'How long do we wait?' Jack asked Tom. He was irritable at having a girl get the drop on him, and inactivity served only to make him more edgy.

'Until we see who rides out on that palomino. Keeler said to look out for one. I'm not going back and 'fessing up to you telling me there's one there without finding out whose it is,' Tom answered, rolling a smoke one-handed while shading his eyes with the other. 'You say the horse was saddled but hadn't been ridden yet?'

'Yes, it was restless, wanted exercising, and wasn't warm or sweating like a mount that had been brought in would be. The saddle and bridle were on, but the saddlebags were thrown across the stall, might not even belong to that horse,' Jack said, then angrily, 'I don't know why Laura Hathersage got so sniffy with me!'

Tom grinned through a blue plume of smoke at Jack. 'Hell, you're sniffy too! Guess that's because you're slipping, Jack, letting a woman creep up and get the drop on you! Anyway, she's all fired up because she admired you some, probably saw you as a future husband, a gentleman with a fine English accent. You don't see so many of those . . . ' He broke off as a sudden realization hit him like lightning from a clear sky, repeated. 'You don't see . . . ' and then laughed quietly to himself.

'What's eating you?' Jack demanded, but Blood remained silent, looking out toward the ranch while finishing his roll-up of Bull Durham.

An hour passed while Jack fretted and Tom impassively watched the distant ranch. Another hour was well under way when Jack exploded. 'I can't stand this damned waiting around!' he said. 'Do we really have to stay here all day behind this pile of rocks, baking and boiling in the heat?'

'You know, Jack,' Tom remarked, still staring outward, 'you are going to have to think about some other kind of job, and I mean that. You have too short a fuse for your own good. It's going to be the undoing of you some . . . ' Again he broke off, then said tersely, 'Rider coming from the ranch. Looks like a palomino that's being ridden.'

'Seems to be a man riding it,' said Jack, shading his eyes. The rider was wearing pants and shirt and a dark sombrero was covering the head.

'Laura Hathersage was wearing breeches back at the ranch,' said Blood, 'and yesterday in town she had a black sombrero.'

Boom! The huge explosion of the Sharps rifle sounded out from the rocks above them, and they saw rider and horse hit the floor in a flurry of dust. As the rider flew over the horse's neck to lie still on the floor the sombrero came off, revealing a flood of blonde hair.

'It *is* her, by God!' Jack shouted, and

running over to his horse he vaulted from a rock into the saddle, snatching the reins over its head and digging his heels into its ribs.

'Cover me!' he shouted, and raced out into the open, towards the fallen horse and rider.

There came the sound of pistol-shots from the rock above, but Blood could neither see nor fire upon those shooting. He swore softly and grabbing up his Henry rifle from the saddle-boot he ran out crablike, hunched over and sideways, rifle held into his hip, scanning the rock face. Bullets were winging out towards Jack as he spurred his mount on, then once more came the boom of the Sharps. Blood fired blindly up at the rock face above him, peppering out the shots to try and gain Jack some time and distance, maybe even force the bushwhackers out. A scrabbling noise and the sound of falling pebbles over to his left told him that the assailants were making off up the rock. He glimpsed a sudden movement above and snapped off a shot. There came a flurry of bullets around him, wild shots designed to make him keep down, but he snapped off another and there came a cry of pain, some confused shouting and then the sound of horses' hooves making off as the gang took flight. Blood turned and looked to see how Jack was doing.

Men from the ranch were kneeling and firing at Jack, who was now lying along the flank of his horse as he galloped to avoid their fire. When he reached Laura and her palomino he saw her lying still next to the dead horse which had taken a massive Sharps bullet clean through the head. She was covered in blood, but as he jumped down and scooped one arm under her, lifting her slightly, he could see that there was no wound to her body, that all the gore came from the horse. It had liberally spattered her, its head virtually destroyed by the speeding bullet which had passed clean through, missing Laura by a matter of inches. She was merely stunned by her fall, Jack saw. Before moving her any further he felt down her legs to see if any bones were broken, then ran his hand inside her shirt to check that no ribs had been smashed in.

'Hold your fire!' he bellowed, crouching down with Laura behind the dead palomino for shelter as bullets continued to wing in from the ranch. 'She's still alive. Do you want to kill her now?'

The shooting stopped and men began to walk warily out towards them. Laura moaned and stirred.

'What?' she asked, then looked up into Jack Storney's eyes.

'You're safe now,' Jack said. 'Your horse was shot from under you, but the gang's been frightened off and you aren't injured. Try to sit up a little.'

Laura came to a sitting position, still leaning against Jack. She put a hand to her face, saw the blood and grimaced; then, with a gasp of embarrassment, saw that her shirt was wide open and her breasts were showing, and began to fasten her buttons hurriedly. Jack looked equally discomfited.

'I beg your pardon,' he said. 'I didn't know how badly injured you were, nor how long you would be unconscious. I had to check for any injuries.'

Laura's face was afire. She swallowed, then said huskily, 'I have to thank you for saving me. Those swine would have put another bullet into me if you had not been there to distract and drive them off, sir.'

At that moment Tom galloped up, just in time to see Laura buttoning her shirt. He grinned at Jack's obvious embarrassment, and winked to compound it.

'Where did you learn to ride like an Apache, on the flank?' he asked Jack.

'At Flagg point-to-point races, back home, when a saddle-girth snapped,' Jack answered.

Men from the ranch rode up, with an

ashen-faced Emory Hathersage, effusive in his thanks.

'Save it,' Blood said. 'Someone look after Miss Hathersage. Leave some men behind to guard the ranch. The rest saddle up and let's ride. I figure I winged one of the scum. Let's see if we can track them and ride the whole gang down.'

In a quarter of an hour a posse of eight men sat atop the rock, looking down on a blood-trail that led up out of the gully.

'Looks like he was dragged up here and put on his mount,' Blood said.

Burt Stevenson, a leathery old wrangler who had organized the ranch-hands, knelt and looked close at the blood.

'This guy's been lung-shot,' he pronounced. 'The blood's deep red, an' look here, where he's spat out froth an' blood. Good shooting.'

'Shouldn't be too long before they have to leave him or turn and fight, then,' said Emory Hathersage. 'Let's ride!'

18

There were seven of them including the dying man, and as Emory Hathersage had predicted they didn't ride far. Nate was slowing them down. The fast pace needed to escape the distant posse they occasionally glimpsed as the trail wound up towards the Steins Mountains was impossible while one of their number had to ride alongside the wounded Nate, holding him into his saddle. Eventually they reached a small canyon which led into the side of the mountain they were ascending. Trees and low bushes masked its mouth, and they halted there, lifting Nate carefully from his saddle.

When he was lying on the ground with an old confederate army slicker laid under him, Fletcher Hawkshaw swung down off his mount and came to kneel at Nate's side. He bit a plug of chewing-baccy off with a clasp-knife, made as if to offer some to Nate, then realized his mistake. Nate was breathing shallow, his face rigid with pain, and from time to time he coughed and spat his lifeblood out on the ground before him.

'Nate, boy, y'hear me?' Fletcher asked. Nate nodded weakly.

'Guess you realize it's all up with you now, Nate,' Fletcher said bluntly. 'That Tom Blood got yer in the lung an' yer fixin' ter die.'

'Ain't gone yet,' Nate said, struggling to stand once more. A paroxysm of coughing gripped him and Fletcher had to support the renegade, hold him up and forward so that he could spit and clear his lungs to breathe again.

'Lookee, Nate, we bein' chased by Blood an' a whole scad of others,' Fletcher said. 'Now, d'you see where we are?'

'Doubtful Canyon,' Nate gasped.

'OK. We can get out, up over the back, but it's gonna take us a while.

We cain't take you with us, an' we need you to hold 'em off a while. D'you think y'can do thet for us, Nate?'

Nate managed a grimace close to a smile. 'Jest set m'Sharps up for me, an I'll take a few t'hell,' he said.

'Had to leave it behind,' Fletcher said, lying smoothly. Damn, but it was enough to lose a man without letting a good rifle go too. 'Don't worry. Just keep loosin' off a pistol-shot from time to time, an' they'll keep their heads down long enough for us to get out o' th' canyon.'

He placed Nate's pistol in his hand and a box of ammunition by his side, patted him on the shoulder, then stood up. For the first time since he came to the valley, he was worried. Who the hell was this Tom Blood?

Some of the other men came over to say their adieus to their old partner. Others, who hadn't fought against the North alongside the Missouri rebel, just let him lay and spurred their mounts on into the canyon, looking nervously back for a last glimpse of the trail and the pursuing posse.

When the last man had gone Nate managed to struggle to a sitting position, his back against the trunk of a ponderosa pine, and clutching his pistol he watched the track before him where the trail veered off into the canyon. Shouldn't be long now. He hoped not; his eyes were beginning to blur and the pain in his back and lungs hurt like hell. Just one, let me take just one of them, he prayed. And if it please you, Lord, let it be Tom Blood.

He was slipping away fast when the sound of the posse's drumming hooves awoke him from a dream. He'd been sitting at home, on a bench outside the cabin with Beau and Earle, while Momma fixed him his favourite meal, chicken-fried steak and collard greens with biscuits, and Beau had yelled for her to put plenty vinegar in with the greens, y'hear me, Maw? He chuckled as the dream faded, and carefully he raised the pistol, gripping it with both hands. As the first dim shape hove into view he took an unsteady aim and fired. The thump of the discharged bullet drove the pistol into his chest, and he gasped with pain and fell sideways, firing the gun into the ground at his side. He saw as he fell that he had hit no-one; he had failed, and as Tom Blood stepped warily up towards him, gun in hand, Nate's last, defiant act of his wasted life was to spit blood onto the gunman's boots.

19

Riding back into town in the late afternoon, chagrined at being so close to the gang only to lose them, Jack said to Tom, 'I don't understand why Keeler should tell us such an obvious lie, about the palomino, I mean. He must have known that we would have found out it was Laura Hathersage's favourite mount.'

'It didn't matter,' said Tom slowly, thinking it out aloud. 'Why do you think the two guys were waiting for us up in the rocks, with that buffalo rifle?'

'Us?' asked Jack. 'But surely . . . You mean Keeler told the gang to knock us off, not Laura Hathersage?'

Blood nodded. 'Of course. We're too near the truth of the thing. If they'd wanted to kill Laura Hathersage they could have done it any time, when she rode into Eden, like the other day, unescorted, or when she was out, exercising her horse. Keeler wanted us dead. He told us to watch out for the palomino in the hopes that we might find it at the ranch, face up to old Hathersage and he would shoot us, or we'd shoot him, and that would start off a war between the railroad and the ranchers and farmers. When the guys who were sent to kill us saw their chance, they decided to get two birds with one stone, shoot Laura Hathersage and make it look as if we'd done it. There we were, hiding in wait for her, just below the rock. Who'd have believed us? We'd have been gunned down or lynched, and the war would have started anyway.'

'I'm looking forward to my next meeting with Keeler,' said Jack grimly.

'Keep your temper,' Blood said. 'We can't prove anything yet. Keeler will just say, well then, there were two palominos, and we're stuck. Today just showed us what I've been saying all along: they're desperate, and they're making mistakes. We're on top of the game. Let's stay that way.'

Entering Eden they saw a crowd of folks blocking the entrance to the alley at the side of the livery stable, and checked their horses.

'What's the excitement?' Jack asked one of the rubberneckers.

The guy snickered nastily. 'Guess you could say ol' Seth had his last long drink.'

'Meaning?' Blood asked the man.

'Why, they just found him near his shack, drowned in one of the livery stable's troughs,' the guy said. 'One drop too many, huh?' He cackled at his own wit.

Blood looked at the man. It was enough. 'Don't be here when I come out the alley,' he said, swinging out of his saddle. The guy remembered business elsewhere. Real urgent business.

Seth was down the end of the alley, round the back of the stables, in an empty corral. He was still head and shoulders down in the green, scummy waters of the trough, his arms resting on the sides.

'Look, I found him, but it ain't my responsibility,' a man was saying to a black-coated dude with the mournful expression of a mortician.

'And I can't bury him till the sheriff's seen the body,' the mortician said. 'He'll be along presently, then you can take him out and see to the funeral. Sheriff won't authorize burial of an old drunk on the town taxes.'

'How come you found Seth?' Tom asked the first speaker.

'Came round to clean the trough out,' the guy said. 'I own the stable and I got horses coming in tomorrow. Corral ain't been used in a while.' He turned to the mortician. 'It ain't right. Just 'cos I let Seth sleep in the old shack, and he dies here. Why should I pay?'

'Ain't my responsibility to bury folks free, either,' the undertaker replied calmly, arms folded. 'We'll wait and see what Dawson says.'

'I told Dawson already. He says he's got better things to do than come and see how the town drunk died,' the livery stable owner answered. '*I say* it's your job to bury the dead.'

Blood looked Seth over where he lay, then gripped the old man firmly but gently under his shoulders and laid him on his back in the dirt. From the swamper's jacket pocket he pulled a three-quarter empty bottle of bourbon. 'How much to bury a man in these parts?' he asked the mortician, putting his hand to his own shirt pocket and bringing out a flat wad of dollars.

'Why, I can do a real cheap funeral for ten dollars,' the man said eagerly.

Blood gave him twenty. 'Make it a decent one,' he said simply.

Jack straightened up from looking closely at Seth's body. He dug out his own poke and gave the mortician a sizeable donation. 'Throw in a few wreaths and a hearse with black horses, will you?' he asked.

'Why, sure, sure,' the man oiled. 'I can guarantee, you'll get a real decent . . . '

Jack waved him away, paid two men to go fetch a litter to carry the corpse over to the mortuary. The excitement over, the crowd drifted away.

'Accident?' Jack asked Blood as they stood by the corpse.

Tom snorted. 'Was it hell! Dawson and his boys did this; wanted folks to think Seth fell in the trough after a drinking-spree.'

'How can you be sure?'

'Take a look at him. What do you see?'

'His shirt collar's nearly torn away,' said Jack. 'It was dirty enough when we met him, but it wasn't torn.'

'Exactly,' Blood nodded. 'He's been held under the water till he drowned. Now, look at the whiskey bottle that was in his pocket. Best bourbon. Seth didn't have a dime when we left him, and the barkeep had refused him credit. And remember what Seth said when I

189

tried to buy him a shot of bourbon?'

'He refused it,' said Jack. 'He preferred rotgut. If he was in the money he would have bought two, three bottles of that cheap poison rather than one bottle of dear whiskey. So why was he killed?'

'For what he knew, the same as Dan Johnson. Seth told us that Johnson and Free and the surveyor, Boyd, had been up the valley, that they'd found something mighty important. Soon as they get back, Boyd's shot and missing, maybe dead by now, Johnson's shot and dead, Free's missing and wanted, and now Seth's dead for talking to us.'

'How can you be sure it was the sheriff and his boys?' Jack asked.

Tom bent over the corpse and showed Jack the burn-marks on Seth's face. 'They got him drunk then tortured him to get him to talk, then they brought him out here, held him down in the trough and drowned him so he couldn't tell anyone else. Look in the trough, over in the corner.'

Jack looked. At the far end bobbed the mangled, sodden stub of one of Mort Green's cigars. 'I am not going to be able to keep away from Dawson and his boys much longer, Tom,' he said savagely.

'Don't worry. They've got plans for you as well,' Tom said. 'Anyway, if things go as I reckon, we should be able to even the score for old Seth pretty soon, maybe even tonight.'

'How so?' Jack asked, brightening up.

'Well,' Tom said thoughtfully. 'Seth was killed for what Dan Johnson told him. Who else did he talk to that night?'

'Amy Croft!' Jack said. 'So they'll need to silence her as well?'

Tom nodded. 'It's my guess.'

'Then she's in danger now!' Jack said. He turned impulsively. 'Let's ride!'

'Stay your hand,' Tom advised. 'That scum does its work in the dark. The

191

Croft place is too public. Someone might see them in the day if they rode out and killed her. Tonight we'll stake the widow's house out, see who comes calling.'

20

As night began to fall Blood and Jack left the saloon, after deliberately letting Mike the barkeep overhear that they were heading out to the rail-camp and would be staying there overnight.

'That should satisfy Dawson. He's bound to ask where we've got to,' Blood said. He had strapped on the twin to the single Smith and Wesson he normally wore, ready for whatever the night brought, and Jack, who 'dearly loved a scrap, old feller,' was raring to go.

The road was clear, they met no-one, and after fifteen minutes at canter pace they reached the widow's farm. There they reined in and surveyed the site with a professional eye, gauging where the intruders might try to break in, and how it might best be defended.

'We'll take them while they're still

outside,' Blood said. 'I don't want any gunplay inside the house.'

'There's a moon rising,' Jack said, turning in his saddle and looking across at the low range of hills behind the farm. 'Should be enough light in an hour or so for us to work by.'

'There's shutters all around the house,' said Blood. 'If we fasten all but one on the ground floor, leave it half open as if Mrs Croft forgot it, then it'll seem like an open invite to them, and we can get them as they try to get in. OK?'

'Then that's the best window to bait them with,' Jack said, as they walked their mounts down from the farm gate. 'That side window. One of us can stake it out from the barn, he can see any approach from behind; and one of us can hide under that big cottonwood over there, he'll be able to see any approach from in front of the house; and once they're at the window, we've both got them covered without getting each other in any crossfire.'

194

They tied up their horses to a rail by the barn and came round to the front of the house. Through an unshuttered window they could see Amy Croft working by the light of an oil-lamp, her face placid as she bent her slender neck over a patch she was sewing onto a garment. By her side lay Fury the mastiff who rose to his feet and stood before her, growling low as he saw them appear at the window. Amy Croft looked up, smiled, and laid down her sewing. She motioned to the front door, and they made their way round.

When Tom and Jack explained the situation to her she watched their lips carefully, nodding in agreement with every stage of their plan, disagreeing only when they suggested that she stay in the house while they guarded it from outside.

'I think that I will spend the night in the barn,' she told them firmly. 'I'll feel safer out of the way.'

Within a few minutes all was set for any visitors. Tom's and Jack's horses were stabled and the widow had retired to the loft in the barn, her dog chained to the ladder, and a Colt's Navy pistol belonging to her dead husband in her grasp. Blood and Jack took up their positions, Tom just inside the barn and Jack fifty yards away below the cottonwood tree, with a full view both up and down the road that ran past the house.

The hours dragged by, and it was just after midnight when Tom saw Jack step out from behind the cottonwood, masked from the road by its trunk, put his thumb up in the moonlight then point up the road towards Eden. He held up two fingers to signify two men approaching, then turned his two fingers down and scissored them back and forth to indicate that the intruders were approaching on foot. Jack waved an arm round the barn door, then the two men stepped back into their hides and waited.

Five minutes later Blood saw through the gap in the barn door two men meet directly opposite him against the back wall of the house. In the moonlight he could clearly see that it was Mort Green and Sam Collins, and Collins was hobbling painfully.

'Jesus!' Collins grumbled. 'I jest about bust my feet up in these damn Injun shoes!'

'They's a window unshuttered here,' Green hissed. 'Gimme your clasp-knife and I'll force the latch.'

Collins handed it over and Green got to work. 'Go walk around that soft ground in your moccassins, leave some prints,' he told Collins, and Collins limped off in the moonlight and carefully left prints to implicate Free. As he returned there was a click and the window swung free with a slight noise.

'Quiet!' Collins warned, and Green gave his nasty snigger.

'She's deaf as a post,' he told his sidekick. 'Gimme that Indian bead-work. I'm gonna leave it at the bottom of the bed when I'm done with her, make it look like Free bust his belt when he pulled his pants up after he'd finished.'

'His pants?' Collins enquired. 'You mean you're going to . . . '

'O' course,' Green said. 'I aim to have me some fun with her first. Gimme a shove up to the ledge.'

'Hey, I want seconds with the widow-woman, 'fore she's killed,' Collins said.

'OK, I'll fetch you,' Green agreed, and the vile deal struck, Collins bent, hands locked, to give Green a boost through the window.

Tom listened, felt his disgust and anger rising, then breathed deep, told himself that it was a feeling he could not afford, that those emotions made a man careless. He felt them go away and be replaced by a determination to cleanse the world of the two abominations before him. Time to do what he was good at.

Blood stepped out, pistols levelled. 'Hey, boys!' he called to the two deputies, and coldly watched Green whip round and make as if to draw. Blood triggered the most perfect killing instruments ever made. Two shots slammed Mort Green back against the house side and two more hit him on the way down. He died before he had time to register the fact.

Tom had left Collins to Jack, as he was the closer of the two deputies, and sure enough a shot hit the crouching deputy, almost as Blood's second volley was smacking into the chest of Green. It was a long shot, however, and Collins was merely wounded in the thigh. Killing defenceless drunks and raping women was more Collins' style and he had no intention of staying to fight. Bent over double he stepped back into the shadow of the house and ran, dragging one leg, for the corner and what he thought was safety.

Tom levelled his gun and was about to take aim at the squat deputy's back when the dark corner of the house seemed to detach itself and step out to meet the fleeing man. Collins gave a scream, then a muffled gurgle as the shape showed itself to be Billy Free, who brought his hand up into the stomach of the man, punched hard and then withdrew his hand. The light of the moon twinkled on the reddened blade of a Bowie knife.

'That's the lot,' Free assured Blood, who was crouched cat-like over his pistols, looking around him in case Dawson had come along for what Green had thought would be fun. The half-breed bent and wiped his knife on Collins' shirt then replaced it in its sheath.

'Where the deuce did you spring from?' Jack asked Billy, nettled that he hadn't made a clean kill, that an outsider had had to step in and finish his business for him.

'He's been here all the time, haven't you, Billy?' Blood said quietly. 'Hiding out in the barn, along with the surveyor, Henry Boyd. He still alive? He was yesterday when we called in. Hope he is, he's got a lot to tell me.'

'You're just guessing,' Billy said with an uneasy laugh. 'How do you know all that?'

'Well, let's see,' said Tom, considering. 'Yesterday when we called Mrs Croft was in the barn, came out with a clean apron on, kind she'd work around the house in, or tend a sick man. She wouldn't have worn it to work in the barn. She'd chained her dog to the wall of the barn to guard the door. Guard a barn? What's she got in there, I wondered, especially when I saw that the hasp and staple that held the dog-chain was new. When we got in the house I saw her brushing the front of her apron clean. Some of it fell on the carpet. It was lint, small threads, kind of stuff you'd get if you were tearing up sheets to make bandages to wrap a wound. Then tonight, when we got here, she's sitting by the window, light on, almost as if to say to anyone looking for you and Henry Boyd, look, I live here alone. If she really was alone a smart woman like her wouldn't be advertising the fact, so I figured you'd still be here, looking out for the lady and your friend Boyd. Now what gives, Billy?'

'Guess I owe you guys an apology,' Billy Free said. 'I didn't know whether we could trust you, being railroad men, but . . . ' he indicated the bodies of the two deputies lying before them, 'you're obviously not in with Keeler and the gang. Come in the barn; it's time to level with you.'

Inside the barn stood Amy Croft, gun in one hand, a lantern in the other. Free moved his lips without speaking, and she watched his face, nodded when he had finished, then turned to Tom and Jack.

'Gentlemen, I am very grateful for the service you did me tonight. Your lives have been in danger because I did not tell you all I knew when you first came to the farm. I am sorry for that, but I had another person's life to protect. If you step this way I will introduce you to him. What he has to say will be of great interest to you, I am sure.'

Blood climbed the open steps up to the loft and waited for Amy Croft, followed by Billy and Jack. Billy moved some bales and a small door was revealed.

'My room,' Billy explained. 'I work on the farm from time to time.'

Blood nodded, and they all stepped through into a little room. Inside it, on a truckle bed, covered with a patchwork quilt, lay a young man, his face pale and drawn. The upper half of his body was swathed in bandages, and he was perspiring freely.

'We daren't fetch Doc Young from town, Dawson would have got wind of it, so I gave him some herbs, other stuff, to kill some of the pain and make him sleep,' Billy whispered. 'He took a bullet in the back, escaping from Keeler, but I dug it out and he's going to be OK, thanks to Mrs Croft.

If she hadn't taken us in, he'd be dead by now.'

'It's the least I could do,' Amy Croft said. 'Keeler and his cronies had my husband killed, and Dan Johnson. I'm glad you're here, Mr Blood, that we've begun to fight back.'

The man in the bed stirred at the sound of voices, then opened his eyes. Tom pulled a rickety chair up to the side of the bed.

'Mr Boyd?' he asked. 'I'm Tom Blood. I reckon you have a lot to tell me.'

21

'So,' Jack said to Tom some time later, standing in the yard with Billy Free, 'what the devil do we do now? Ride into the rail-camp and confront Keeler with what we know?'

'No,' said Tom, thoughtfully. 'That won't lead us to who's behind Keeler, nor to the gang, and I want both.'

'How do we do that?'

'I guess it's time to apply a little pressure to Sheriff Dawson,' Tom replied, pointing to the two deputies, still lying where they'd been dropped. 'Let's go find these two's horses. We've got something to deliver before daybreak.'

Half a mile down the road Billy located the deputies' mounts and trotted them back to the farm. Once there the three men worked at lashing the corpses belly-down over their saddles, then riding beside the laden horses they took them through the night towards Eden.

Just outside the town they whipped up the dead men's horses and let them gallop alone into town. From the shelter of a derelict barn they watched the horses and their macabre burdens slow to a trot as they neared the sheriff's office and come to a halt by the hitching-rail. A light at the office window showed that Dawson was in, waiting for his deputies to return. Eventually one of the horses, growing restless, whinnied, and the sheriff stepped out onto the front porch, a lantern in his hand. He took one look at the scene before him, dropped the lantern, then bolted back inside the office.

'Now what?' Jack asked.

'He's on his own in Eden now. If I got the man's measure he'll run for whoever's been giving him orders,' Tom answered quietly, 'see what to do next.'

'And he'll run to Keeler or the gang,' Billy said.

'Any price you like it'll be Keeler,' Tom said, 'and he's going to bolt soon. He'll be afraid whoever killed his deputies will come after him next.'

No more than five minutes had passed when an agitated Dawson erupted from his office. He held in one hand his rifle and a tote-bag, and in the other a bed-roll. He loosened the ropes that bound Collins to his horse, and the body fell into the dirt. Dawson stashed his belongings on the horse, scrambled into the saddle and pulling savagely at its head spurred it out of town. He rode towards them, but looped off before reaching where they kept watch, heading overland for the rail-camp.

'He's scared someone's waiting for him along the trail,' said Billy.

'He's right,' said Blood. 'Can we get to the rail-camp ahead of him?'

'Oh, sure,' said Billy. 'He's looping round to avoid the trail. We can cut off a mile or so down the way and then go straight across country. Just follow me.'

They rode steadily for half an hour, and the first light of day was beginning to streak the eastern sky when Billy Free held up a hand and reined them in. 'We're about half a mile from the rail-camp now,' he said. 'They've got a couple of guards out since the pay-roll robbery. We'll have to leave the horses and walk in.'

They tied the horses up under a clump of trees and followed a small dry wash for a half mile or so, then came out on a low ridge above a camp of orderly rows of tents. A locomotive bestrode the rails that ended abruptly a hundred yards further on, its stack showing the occasional spark and wisp of smoke as the daylight increased. On a temporary spur line some distance from the tents stood a passenger coach, with no lights showing at the windows.

'That'll be Keeler's office and sleeping-quarters,' Jack said as the three lay atop the ridge, looking down.

'Here comes a rider, too,' said Billy, pointing to his right, and in the distance could be seen a lone horseman making a good pace, dust-clouds spurting up behind his mount's hooves. They heard a shouted challenge, saw the horse slow to a walk as its rider identified himself to the concealed guard, then trot on up to the wagon.

'That's Dawson,' said Jack. 'He's riding a bay with a white blaze.'

'I'd like to be down there,' Blood told Billy. 'Reckon we can do it?'

Billy considered, head on one side, looking along the ridge. 'We can do it,' he said, 'but we need to go along to our left a piece, come out back of the wagon. One of us can stay some distance away, keep a rifle trained on the area in case we have to light out fast.'

'Guess who?' said Jack with a smile, unshipping a Winchester from his saddle-boot.

It took five minutes to scramble and

crawl to a place where Billy and Tom
could run crouched-over to stand by
the side of the railroad coach. Inside
could be heard the raised voice of Jake
Dawson.

'It's got to be Blood and that damned
English guy, I tell yer,' Dawson was
bleating. 'They said they was coming
to the camp, and they ain't here. They
must have got wind of my plan and
staked the widder's house out for Mort
an' Sam.'

Silence for a while, and then Keeler's
elegant tones: 'Damn it, but you're
right. The game's up, and if we want
to save our own necks we'd do best to
get out.'

'Where to?' Dawson asked, fear in
his voice.

'Only one place,' Keeler answered.
'We make a meet with Fletcher and
the boys, and light out of the territory
together. Once we're safe away, we split
from them.'

'And the pay-roll?'

Keeler's voice grew smoother. 'Well,

with Collins and Green out of the action, we split it two ways when we're clear.'

'Now it ain't that I don't trust yer,' came Dawson's voice, 'but what's to stop yer puttin' a bullet in me once we're on our way to meet up with the gang, and keepin' it all for yerself? Fletcher don't know about the pay-roll, does he?'

'Because until we meet up with the gang, I need you to cover my back, and you need me to do the same,' Keeler was explaining patiently. 'We could be tracked, have you thought of that? If Blood's this good he could be on our tail right now!'

Billy took his head from the carriage side and smiled at Tom, who unshipped a gun in case the sheriff decided to check.

'OK, that makes sense,' Dawson agreed grudgingly, 'but I'm gonna be watchin' you all the way, Keeler. Don't try anything on me. Where we meeting up with Hawkshaw and the gang?'

'We make for Broken Ridge and light a fire. They're due to check the place tomorrow evening for any instructions. We see Fletcher, and he'll give us an escort clear down to the Mexican border. We need to lie low for a while, wait till we're contacted, and then we'll get our split out of the contract money. It's that simple, Dawson. Don't worry, man.'

'Let's get out now, then,' Dawson urged, real fear in his voice. 'I don't feel safe round here any more. That Blood's somethin' else!'

'Yes,' came Keeler's voice as the two of them stepped out of the carriage and walked down the steps. 'Blood's ruined everything here. I'd like a few minutes with the man!'

'I'll try to oblige,' Blood muttered as he and Billy ran back to where Jack was waiting. When they were safely under cover again he asked Billy, 'This Broken Ridge Keeler was talking about? You know where it is?'

'Yeah,' said Billy. 'I can take you

212

there. Be about three hours' ride. When do we go?'

Blood thought for a moment. 'When we go, we need to go team-handed,' he said. 'We're going to have to take that gang on, too, and finish them for good and all. Who can we trust, Billy?'

'Emory Hathersage and his hands,' Billy said promptly. 'The gang tried to kill Laura. They know we've got to clean the valley of them, and they'll trust you.'

'Right,' said Blood. 'We'll get Hathersage to make up a posse for us. Let's head for the Circle A.'

22

Riding out to the Circle A, Tom let Billy draw ahead, then rode alongside Jack. 'OK, Jack,' he said, 'spit it out.'

'I don't foller, old chap,' Jack said, but he could not meet Tom's eye.

'Something's been chewing on you since we left the widow's place,' Tom said patiently, 'and I want it cleared before we come up against Fletcher and the gang.'

'Hell's teeth!' Jack suddenly exploded. 'Why didn't you tell me all that stuff about Free and Boyd, and knowing where they were all along? I felt so damned stupid! I thought we were partners until you came out with all that about lint on her apron and . . . and . . . and the bloody hound chained to the barn! And when Boyd told us his story and you said you'd suspected it for some time . . . ' He broke off, almost spluttering with anger.

'What good would it have done you?' Tom asked.

'I would have *known*!' Jack shouted, yanking on his reins. 'We're supposed to be partners!'

Tom rode awhile, then said, 'Jack, you're a good guy, and I've ridden for a time with you now. I ask for none better in a tight corner. You've guts and skill with a gun. But I told you before, you're not cut out for this. Sooner rather than later you're going to end up dead, because you take it all too personal, and you still think the whole thing's a big adventure. If I'd told you back there what my suspicions were, of who was behind Keeler and the gang, you would have let your feelings get in the way of the job, and you would have made your play too early.'

Jack grunted, his face set. He knew Tom was right.

'I tell you again, Jack,' Tom said. 'Get out of this game while you can. You're young and you're fast, and

215

you're getting a reputation. But coming up behind you is someone younger and faster, and he wants your reputation off of you, he wants to be known in every rail-town as the man who nailed Jack Storney. And *that* guy will have a cooler head than yours. That will be his edge — and your funeral.'

'Point taken, Tom,' Jack said with a rueful smile. 'God, but I wish Farley was riding with us on this one.'

Wisely, Tom said nothing, but kept his suspicions to himself.

★ ★ ★

Jack could not guess but Farley was indeed riding with them on this one. Travelling hard and fast he had reached the valley the day before, and then circled around to get the feel of the situation, avoiding Eden and the rail-camp for fear of coming across Jack and Tom.

At first it was in his mind to find Fletcher and warn him of the calibre of man he was up against in Tom Blood. As he rode deeper into the valley, however, Farley's mood grew sombre, for instead of meeting the usual hospitality at the small farms and ranches he chanced across he was ordered off, sometimes at the point of a gun. From some of the wary settlers he heard of the atrocities of the murderous gang Fletcher commanded. It was when he sat his horse and looked at the burnt-out remains of Wood Linkin's farm, saw the four humped mounds, two full-size, two pathetically small, that were the graves of the farmer, his wife and children, silent witnesses to the bloody deeds of the animals he had hoped to reason with, that a conviction grew in his mind. He knew now that the South was dead, that these murdering criminals had to be killed as one would kill a pack of rabid dogs, as much for their sakes as that of the community they preyed on.

'Tom was right,' he murmured to

himself. 'The old days sure are done with.'

A seasoned guerrilla fighter who knew instinctively the ways of the men he hunted, Farley wasted neither time nor energy in a fruitless search for Fletcher and his accomplices, but instead sought out the kind of broken country he knew they would hide out in, and then waited for them to find him. He had no plan, just a burning desire to wipe out the shame they had brought on the South he loved.

* * *

As they approached the Hathersage spread Tom remarked to the others that it looked deserted. They reined in close to, then saw Laura Hathersage accompanied by the yellow dog come around the corner of the hacienda, carrying a rifle loosely under her arm. She raised a hand to her eyes, then, recognizing the three riders, waved them in.

'Where is everybody?' Tom asked abruptly as he slid from his mount.

'Gone on round-up,' she forced out. You could tell it was still hurting her to be sociable to Tom, though she turned a pole-axing smile on Jack and continued her conversation through him. 'Dad's taken all but six of the men up the valley to drive the cattle down and brand them here. Should be back in five or six days.'

'Your father has gone on round-up?' Jack asked incredulously. The first time they'd met the old feller he wouldn't have ridden anything but his rocking-chair.

'Yes,' she said happily. 'Looks like the gang trying to kill me has given him some sand. I offered to take the men, but Pa said it was his job as ranch-boss. He's even hoping to flush the gang out, says if they try to take him and the men on, he'll give them a whupping! But what brings you up here, with Billy?'

Briefly Jack explained to Laura that

they were hoping to raise a posse to track and crush the gang for good.

'But you'll still have a posse,' Laura said, her blue eyes lighting up. 'I'll bring four of the men and leave two behind to guard the ranch. That should be enough, makes eight of us.'

'Seven,' said Jack firmly. 'I could not permit you to ride into any more danger, Miss Hathersage.'

'It's not up to you,' Laura told him, the steel coming into her voice. 'This is my father's ranch, and my father's ranch-hands that you need to trap the gang. My father and mother settled this valley, my brother Frank died for it and is buried yonder, next to Ma. Hathersage sweat and blood is on this land. One day this spread will be mine, and I wouldn't be worthy of it if I let others do my dirty work for me.'

'Don't look at me,' Blood said as Jack turned to him for support.

'Then that's settled,' Laura said briskly. 'I'll go pick four of the men and we'll be ready in ten minutes, if you are.'

Blood tipped his hat, gave a little smile as she walked away, but Jack exploded.

'She is the most headstrong, impulsive, argumentative . . . ' he said, then stopped, red-faced and lost for words.

'Wonder who she 'minds me of?' Tom said, with a slight smile, still watching Laura go. 'Good figure, though, you have to allow. Still, you'd know better than me, eh, Jack, having seen more of it?'

Jack's reply was unsuited to an English gentleman.

23

It was mid-afternoon when Billy Free reined in the posse. They had ridden for almost four hours, and for the last hour had been strung out, carefully following the tracks of Keeler and Dawson, the half-breed scouting ahead at times, making sure that they did not give themselves away, nor stumble upon the two men unawares.

'Broken Ridge's about two mile away,' Billy said to Tom, pointing to a low ridge ahead, rising up out of the underbrush. 'Now, how d'you want to handle this?'

Blood chewed his lip while he considered. 'We can't wait here and track them when they rendezvous with the gang,' he said, 'because we could lose them once they get up in those hills beyond, or they could bushwhack us when we follow. We need to take

Dawson and Keeler out of it, then lay in wait for the gang.'

Billy grunted agreement, then said, 'OK. You and Jack follow me on foot. I can get close enough to take those two, but we need to be quiet.'

Leaving Laura and the posse concealed in the brush Billy led them forward. After travelling cautiously for a couple of miles he motioned for Tom and Jack to stay where they were and, crouching low, he made off to one side of the ridge. Half an hour later he was back.

'I found them,' he said. 'Follow me.' Even as he spoke there came the sharp crack of a rifle-shot close by. Billy looked startled then spun round and made off at a trot, followed by Tom and Jack. The half-breed led them close to the edge of a small clearing at the base of the ridge, crawled the last few yards to the cover of an outcrop of rock, then carefully peered round it. After a couple of minutes he waved Tom and Jack to do likewise.

In the clearing were Keeler and Dawson. Their horses were tied to the low branch of a cottonwood, and a small fire burnt in the centre of the clearing. The two men were kneeling over a freshly-killed young maverick steer they had chanced across and which one of them had obviously just shot with a rifle which lay by it. Dawson had a knife in his hand and was in the process of cutting some meat off its flank.

'Couple of hours time we'll put green stuff on the fire, send up smoke they'll see from the top of the ridge. Be three hours or so before they get here,' Keeler was saying to Dawson. 'It would have been a shame to sit here with our bellies growling.'

'I guess this is one of Hathersage's beeves,' Dawson said, threading a couple of fair-sized steaks on a green branch to roast over the fire. 'Only right he should give us our last feed in the valley!'

Tom signalled to Billy and Jack and

the three withdrew a safe distance from the clearing.

'I need Keeler alive,' Tom told Billy. 'If we go rushing in there the chances are he might be killed in the gunplay we'll get into and then I'll never know who's behind all this. Do you think you can take Dawson out of it and get Keeler for me?'

'Nothing to it,' Billy told Tom. 'Just watch them from the rocks and leave it to me.' He turned and disappeared silently into the undergrowth. Jack and Tom crept back to the rocks and watched Keeler tending the fire while Dawson cut down green branches to make a signal-fire later.

Five minutes passed, then ten. Keeler was walking back across the clearing to add to the pile of greenstuff for the signal-fire when Billy appeared on the rocks behind him. The Apache 'breed's arm was drawn back; he whipped it down, pointing directly at the crooked sheriff's back, and a silver blur flew from his hand across the clearing to lodge in Dawson's back. A look of surprise then agony crossed Dawson's face. He dropped the sticks with a scream of pain, clawed with his right hand at his back, then pitched forward at Keeler's feet, blood trickling from his mouth.

Startled, Keeler made as if to rise, one hand reaching below his jacket for his gun, but even as he made it to his knees Billy Free leaped across the clearing like a cougar. Halfway across the clearing he launched himself forward and struck Keeler with his left shoulder square in the chest. Billy bore the engineer back down to the floor where he expertly turned the winded man over and held his arms behind him, grinding Keeler's face into the dirt.

When Keeler had stopped gasping for breath he saw Blood squatting over him.

'Now,' Blood said, and his voice was cold and without pity. 'You're going to talk to me, Keeler. I know what Henry

Boyd and Dan Johnson found when Free here took them up the valley. You are going to tell me the rest; who your boss is, where the money goes, that kind of stuff.'

'You can rot in hell,' Keeler gasped. 'When Hasland Coldwell hears of this . . . '

'Don't try to bluff me; you're in no position. I know you're fixing to get out the valley with the gang Coldwell sent me to fix. Now talk!'

'Perhaps he's hoping to hold out till Fletcher and his merry men get here,' Jack suggested.

'But you haven't sent the signal yet, have you, Keeler?' Blood asked. 'And we aren't going to send it till we're ready for them. In the meantime you are going to spill your guts to me.'

Keeler sneered and remained silent, and over his body Billy Free looked at Tom, then pointed silently at himself questioningly. Tom nodded, stood aside. Free produced a length of twine from his pocket and lashed

Keeler's hands together behind his back by the thumbs, bringing grunts of pain from his victim. When Free had finished he rose leisurely to his feet and looked down on Keeler.

'You know me?' he asked Keeler, placing his moccasined foot on the back of the engineer's neck and pressing his face down into the dirt, rolled his face back and forward in the grit. Keeler spat out the filth and glowered out of the corner of one eye at Free.

'You're one dead Injun when I get . . .'

'Oh, but you ain't going to get anything you want,' Free interrupted, turning Keeler over with his foot and kneeling on his windpipe before continuing. 'You see, you're my meat now. Blood's handed you over to me. You killed my friend, Dan Johnson. You tried to have me killed, and you sent your dirty little dogs against the widow Croft. They were aiming to rape and kill her, Keeler, put the blame on me. Was that your idea?'

Keeler's face was purple with restricted breathing; he could not answer. Free eased up a mite, then pressed again.

'Well, no matter,' said Free pleasantly. 'I got all afternoon, all night. You're beyond the white man's law now. I aim to give you some Apache justice. You're going to beg me to kill you before I'm finished, Keeler. You just lay there a while till I got everything ready. Got to get the fire nice and hot first.'

'Blood? You going to let this savage torture me?' Keeler asked, fear beginning to show in his face.

'Out of my hands,' Blood said, then turned to Jack and asked him to go and bring the posse up.

When Jack returned with the four men and Laura Hathersage in tow Billy Free had made ready. The camp-fire was blazing up and he had skinned the beast Keeler and Dawson had shot. With the wet hide in one hand and a length of knotted sinews in the other he approached Keeler once more, and squatted by his side.

'Now,' he said pleasantly, conversationally. 'You are probably asking yourself what's that damned savage going to do with one new piece of rawhide and a length of sinew, you not being a cattleman, or used to Injun ways. Weeell, I'll tell you, Mr Keeler . . .'

Here Free broke off to lift Keeler forward and up by his flowing silver hair. With the man's arms still pinioned behind him, he slapped the 'green' hide around Keeler's body, bringing the two ends over on to his chest. He pushed him down and brought out his knife, and Keeler's eyes widened in alarm.

'Oh, don't fret yourself,' Billy assured him. 'I'm not going to scalp you . . . yet. I'm just going to put some holes in the edges here and lace you up inside the hide, like so.'

Within five minutes Keeler was cocooned inside a corset of rawhide. Free seized the helpless man's feet and dragged him over to the fire, watched by the entire posse and a fascinated Laura Hathersage.

'Now,' Billy said, 'any cattleman will tell you that when rawhide is first dried, it shrinks one hell of a lot. I'd advise you to breathe in as far as you can, Keeler, 'cos this is going to pinch, and then some!'

'Damn you!' Keeler shouted, then lay still, but as the constricting grip of the drying hide began to squeeze painfully he started to beg.

'Blood, Storney, you men, for God's sake release me! Don't leave me in this bloody savage's hands! Oh, God!' He broke down and began to sob.

'That's far enough,' said Burt Stevenson, the wrangler from the Circle A. He stepped forward with a clasp-knife to cut Keeler free from his bonds. As he did so, there was a crack and Laura Hathersage whipped the knife out of his hand with the quirt she carried strapped to her right wrist.

'The next man who tries to interfere, I'll shoot,' Laura said as Stevenson rubbed his wrist. She walked over to where Keeler lay by the fire and, reaching down to the pile of greasewood, threw a couple more pieces on, stirring the blaze with her booted foot. Keeler was in agony, and she looked down on him, her lips slightly parted and a look of intense, private pleasure on her face. Keeler squirmed, then cried out with the pain of moving against the rawhide that was literally crushing the life out of him.

'Have pity, ma'am,' Keeler begged her when he saw her standing over him.

'And how much pity did you have on Dan Johnson, or on Wood Linkin and his family? I could name you a dozen more whose deaths are down to you, Keeler,' Laura said, a cold smile on her face. She leaned over closer to him, licked her lips and gave a slight shiver. 'So scream a lot for me, Keeler, please, because I'm loving this. I'm going to watch you die, and damn you to hell when you do!'

Free threw yet more wood on the fire, moved Keeler even closer to the blaze, and when the trussed and tortured man saw that he really was going to be crushed to death with not a single hand lifted to save him, he began to talk. Blood and the rest listened, and with occasional prompts from Blood and Storney, the whole crooked, filthy story was spilt out for the first time.

24

Lon Sleaford found Farley no more than an hour after he had made camp. The tall and skinny ex-confederate scout had lost none of his cunning, sliding up behind Farley and sticking a gun in his ribs while Farley was sipping a mug of coffee. Farley had heard Lon's stealthy approach and it was all he could do to keep steady, given what he knew about the gang's reputation for killing out of hand. When the gun barrel dug in his back he did as Lon said, dropped the mug and stood slowly, his arms held high in the air. As he turned to face Lon he was recognized.

'Farley Bodeen!' Sleaford gasped. 'Boy, I thought you was long gone to Jordan's shore! What you doin' here?' He holstered his gun and grabbed Bodeen's hand, pumping it up and down and pummelling his shoulder with his free hand.

'Was up north, round Missoula, operatin' with Fletcher's cousin . . .' Farley began.

'Jed and the boys are here?' Lon asked eagerly. 'We sure could do with some help right now.'

'No,' Farley said. He looked at Lon's long, sorrowful face, alight with friendship and felt a pang of guilt at deceiving an old comrade-in-arms. 'They right busy up there, but I fancied me a change of scenery and a parley with Fletcher, so I come down, brung him back his luck-piece.' He dug in his pocket and showed the outlaw the musket-ball and button he had palmed at Missoula.

'Ol' Fletcher sure will be pleased to see thet,' Lon said. 'Tho' he'll be powerful disappointed Jed ain't come down. How is Jed?'

'He and the boys was best they been for a while when I left,' Farley said, reflecting that it wasn't exactly a lie.

'Well, come on,' said Lon, holstering his gun. 'I'll bring you to Fletcher and the boys. He'll be mighty pleased to see you. You was at Dexter's Crossing when he got that minney-ball in his chest, worn't you?'

'Ridin' right alongside him,' Farley answered, swinging into his saddle. 'What you doin' out here, riding alone?'

'Oh, I'm jest keepin' watch for a signal-fire, this side of the ridge. We supposed to meet up tonight with the guy who gives Fletcher his orders,' Lon said. 'Come on, our camp ain't far off.'

They rode up Broken Ridge, crested it, then down the other side. Approaching a small knoll, Lon reined in, stroked his lantern jaw, and then said nervously, 'You might find Fletcher a mite changed since you see'd him last, Farley.'

'How d'you mean, Lon?'

'Well, times ain't been easy, an' we all had to do some things we ain't been happy with since we quit the South. 'Cept Fletcher. He's turned real mean. Seems to be enjoyin' the work a shade more than is good for a body. Talk soft to him when you see him. He got one hell of a temper on him too, these days.'

'Thanks for the warning,' Farley said. He dropped slightly back as Lon dug his knees into his horse's flank to urge him on. From his saddlebag he stealthily drew out a small Colt House pistol. It packed only four .41 bullets, and was favoured by gamblers, whores and the rest of the so-called 'sporting' fraternity, but it was a handy little weapon that had saved Farley's neck before. This felt like another time. He stashed it inside his shirt where it lay cold and snug against his skin.

The camp was up against the knoll, and in parts it had been dug into the earth and camouflaged. As Farley rode in and dismounted he saw Fletcher Hawkshaw lying by the fire, his massive frame covered to the chin with a couple of horse-blankets, his shoulders propped against a saddle for a pillow. He turned his mutilated, scarred head and surveyed Farley and Lon through his one good eye, then reached out and took a slug from a bottle of whiskey.

'He's drinkin' to kill off a fever he's took,' Lon whispered, 'though he drinks most the time lately.' Then raising his voice, he hollered, 'Fletcher! Brung yer company from down home!'

'Ain't no need to shout, ain't deef,' Hawkshaw snapped. He looked Farley up and down, then yelled, 'Boys! Come here an' greet a neighbour!'

From a lean-to shelter emerged, blinking and stretching, little, deadly Moss Rogers. Behind him shambled the huge Joe Downes and his cousin the dapper Davey Fields, always smiling. From his lookout's place on the steep slope of the hillside slid a fourth man, his arms crossed over a rifle he held to his chest. Farley did not recognize him, but nodded in his direction after greeting the others.

'You know all the other guys; yon's Jesse Allen,' Fletcher said, and Jesse nodded curtly back to Farley, his eyes cold and watchful.

'So,' Fletcher resumed. 'Good t'see yer, Farley. Been a while since we rid tergither, boy.'

'Surely has,' Farley agreed. 'I bin up Missoula way, with yer cousin Jed, robbing the ol' North Pacific, an' when I got yer note an' Jed said he figgered he'd stay awhile longer I come down to try my luck with you. Brung yer this back.' Farley brought out the button wrapped around a musket-ball, tossed it over to Fletcher, who made no attempt to catch it, but kept his right hand below the blankets.

Fletcher gazed down at his returned luck-piece, then back at Farley. 'So how is my cousin, Farley?' he asked.

'Looked fine when I seen him last,' Farley smiled, feeling something was going very wrong here.

'We surely could do with his help right now. Been havin' a peck of trouble with a pistolero called Blood. Ever hear thet name, Farley?'

Farley pretended to consider, then said, 'No, cain't say as I have.'

'Now that is tolerable strange,' Hawkshaw said, and he nodded to the men standing behind Farley, then looked towards Jesse Allen. 'Y'know, Farley, I ain't never bin one for book-learnin', cain't read or figger too well — took me th' best part of an hour to write thet note to cousin Jed I sent with my ol' luck-piece. But Jesse here, why, he's a wonder, a pure wonder at readin' an' sech, ain't yer, Jesse?' Jesse nodded, and Fletcher said, 'Now, read him that piece from the newspaper Keeler give us the other day, will yer, Jesse?' Fletcher smiled pleasantly at Farley, making the scar stand out more lividly. He reached out for the whiskey bottle with his left hand and took another sip. 'You won't have seen this, I reckon, Farley, but you gonna love it! Ol' Jesse was jest sittin' up there on lookout, half an hour ago, an' readin' at the paper to pass the time, when he see'd this an' he brung it down an' read it to me. Read it, Jesse, will ya?'

From his back pocket Jesse brought out a copy of the *Eden Times* and began to read the account of the gunfight aboard the *Old Independent*.

'Got to say you surprise me, Farley,' Fletcher said, interrupting Jesse. 'Never had you down fer a preacher-man.'

'That paper just ain't true,' Farley protested, and reached inside his shirt. 'Why, I got a letter here from yer cousin Jed . . . '

'Farley, I swear, you as full of shit as a pig in a melon-patch,' Fletcher said, and shot Bodeen with the .45 he'd been nursing under the blanket since Lon and Farley had first ridden into camp.

The lead slug bit into Farley's left shoulder and spun him round, and for a moment he almost fell, but as Fletcher pumped another at him, missing, he ran straight at the gang-leader, whipping from his shirt the small Colt. With a spring he landed on Hawkshaw's body and, stooping with the Colt extended, shot directly into his mask of a face, the bullet entering just below Fletcher's eyepatch, exiting at the back of his skull into the saddle and killing him instantly. Straightening up, Farley saw the startled Jesse Allen barring his only way of escape. Jesse let the newspaper fall and snatched up his rifle, but Farley ran directly at him, giving a rebel yell, and put two bullets in short order into Allen's chest, watching him fall back as Bodeen sprang past and made up the incline to an outcrop of rocks that offered cover. A second bullet took him high in the back, but he grunted with pain, kept his feet, and ran for the heights above him, dropping the Colt that had done its work and pulling from its holster his .45.

Behind, all was confusion. Lon Sleaford was still gaping, not able to believe what he was seeing, while the other guys, who had been aware of Bodeen's treachery when Jesse had first read the paper to them, were pulling iron but getting in each other's way. Moss Rogers, who never missed a chance to shoot a man, had got one into Farley's back, but then Davey Fields spun and knocked the gun from his grasp and he had to shove the great bulk of Joe Downes out of his line of fire before he could get a second bead on Bodeen. Each of the outlaws got off two, maybe three more shots, but missed each time, then their target rolled behind some stunted cedar trees and rocks above them and began returning fire that was pretty damned accurate for seeing how much lead he had already collected. They scattered and took cover, leaving their dead leader lying between them, looking almost as if he was asleep, were it not for the huge red patch that covered one half of his face.

25

Keeler had finished talking and had been released from his rawhide death-wrap. He lay where Free had let him fall, still with his hands bound behind him, and glowered at his captors. The game wasn't up yet, he thought. This bunch had Fletcher Hawkshaw and his boys to deal with, and those Southerners were tough hombres. He would be rescued, then he would make sure that no-one left this place alive to repeat what he had been forced to tell them. That Indian would die real slow too, and as for that Hathersage bitch . . .

Tom was about to throw the green sage-branches that Dawson had cut onto the fire as a signal to the gang, when the sound of distant firing came clearly to them all.

'Coming from that way,' said Billy,

pointing to the north-east.

'What's out there?' asked Blood, straining his eyes but seeing nothing but brush and rock rising up to Broken Ridge.

'Nothing,' said Billy. He cocked his head and listened, then said, 'It sounds muffled, comes and goes with the wind. Could be over the ridge.'

'Sounds like someone's putting up a hell of a fight,' said Jack, coming to stand by them.

'Let's go see,' said Tom. 'Could be Hawkshaw and his crew. We know they're in the area or Keeler and Dawson wouldn't have been here.'

'What about him?' Billy asked, nodding to Keeler lying nearby.

'We need him to take back with us,' Blood said. 'He's going to tell his story one more time, and then he'll stand trial and swing for all the killings that he ordered. Tie his legs and we'll fetch him later. Let's move. Hawkshaw could be killing more innocent folk right now.'

Billy picked up a piece of sinew he had used to lace the rawhide around Keeler and tied the chief engineer's legs securely together. He hauled him up and stuck him against the trunk of a cedar, then knelt close and stared into his eyes, whispered almost lovingly to him.

'Now, that was a white man talking. Shall I tell you what I'm going to do if he don't make it, or he changes his mind? I'm coming back for you, Keeler, and I'm going to show you that Apache justice is just as thorough, but one hell of a sight slower and more painful. Think about it while you're lying there. Pray Blood makes it back and you only hang!'

When the posse had galloped off Keeler tugged and pulled at his bonds, but they were firmly tied. He thought about backing up to the fire and holding his hands in until the twine burnt off, but he knew the pain would be too much to bear. A rocky outcrop beyond the clearing caught his eye. That would do! He'd work his way over there and find a sharp edge against which to rub the twine which secured his hands.

Slowly and painfully he squirmed and hunched his body over to the rocks. It took a while and he was exhausted by the time he made it, his stomach muscles on fire with the work they had to do to propel him across the clearing. His arms were a mass of throbbing pain, but he smiled grimly to himself. His horse and Dawson's were still tied to a tree nearby. Once he was free he would make it out of the valley, get help and come back for his revenge. Now, where . . . ah, yes, ideal! A crevice in the rock had a sharp edge that should cut through the twine. He backed up to it and inserted his bound hands inside the hole, feeling around for the edge.

Inside the crack in the rock the bull rattlesnake stirred and unfolded its coils. Two hours earlier it had been sunning itself on the ledge when the vibrations from booted feet and horses' hooves had driven it to take refuge here. There was little room between the rocks for its four-foot body, and now an intruder threatened. The flat head drew back, the mouth opened and it flicked out its tongue. A heat-sensitive 'eye' between the rattler's nose and eyes detected the warmth from Keeler's questing hands; angrily it shook the rattles on its tail, but Keeler was scrabbling with his boots on the floor outside to gain more leverage and did not hear. The hinged fangs came down from the roof of the snake's mouth, its head shot forward and it struck. There was a sudden scream, the hands were swiftly withdrawn and the rattler slowly subsided, sank back into its coils, impervious to the man who thrashed around in his death throes outside.

★ ★ ★

Cresting the ridge the posse could hear plainly the shooting which had settled down now to a steady sniping-duel. As they neared the outlaws' camp they saw smoke and the flash of fire from a gun muzzle coming from up on the knoll, and three men circling, shouting advice and directions to each other, trying to get up to the man who was firing down. When they heard the sound of horses the men turned and began firing at the posse. Eight guns pounded back in reply and the three fell dead or dying amongst the sage and juniper bushes. From the posse's left a fourth man, a tall, skinny man, broke cover on a horse and galloped off. Laura Hathersage unshipped a Winchester from its saddle-boot, stood in her stirrups and taking a careful bead on the fugitive, coolly pumped two shots into his back. He fell from his horse and was still. The Hawkshaw mob was history.

'You up there!' Blood shouted. 'Friends here. The name's Tom Blood. Throw out your gun and come down. You're safe.'

'Tom,' came a weak shout, 'this is

Farley. Come on up. I cain't make it down.'

Tom and Jack climbed the slope to find Farley propped against the side of the knoll, his gun by his side. He was bleeding from the mouth and his eyes were glazed with pain, but he managed a weak smile.

'Hi, y'all,' he whispered. 'Right pleased to see you fellers!'

'What the deuce happened here?' Jack asked as Tom checked Farley's wounds.

'Weeel, I figgered the South should clean up its own mess,' Farley answered. 'Cain't have folk saying we all tarred with the same brush.'

'Rest easy, boy,' Tom said gently. 'We'll get you down in a while.'

'No, Tom,' Farley coughed. 'It's all up with me, I reckon. Took one in the lung and I'm done fer. Tom, I lied to you, an' I'm sorry. I knowed Fletcher Hawkshaw from way back.'

'I know,' said Tom. 'I knew all along, Farley.'

'Then why didn't y'say?' Farley asked.

'I guess I thought you had to sort it out in your own way, you and your southern pride,' Tom said, forcing a smile.

'Hell, well as my ma used ter say, you smarter'n a bullwhip, Tom Blood. I'm right proud to have rid with yer.'

'Been proud to have you alongside of me,' Tom said, and he gripped Farley's right hand as he died and his soul sped towards his beloved Southland.

26

Once more the president's private train stood waiting in the Fresno railyard for Tom and Jack, once more Lee Chi stood waiting to greet them. This time, however, there was no dispute about weapons.

'You keep guns,' he informed them. 'Mister Coldwell waiting inside. Please come.' He bowed them onto the platform of the train, then held up his hand. 'Please, where third man, your friend who so rude to Lee Chi, call me dwarf?'

'He's dead,' Blood said flatly.

'Ah,' Lee Chi breathed. 'He killed?'

'Yes, shot.'

Lee Chi absorbed the information, then said, 'You come,' and led them inside the president's carriage.

Inside, Hasland J. Coldwell sat at his desk, still looking like a skeleton with a wing collar. His thin hands played with a sheaf of papers. Pacing the carriage, looking ill at ease, was his elegant brother-in-law, Edward Somersby.

'Ah, Mr Blood and Mr Storney,' Coldwell whispered in his dry, dead voice. 'Welcome, and well done. I thought it only polite to come halfway to greet you, thank you for your sterling service, and receive your full report.'

'Yes, indeed, well done,' Somersby added with a forced air of heartiness. 'Killed the whole gang, I hear. Well done, indeed.' He extended his hand.

'There's still one at liberty,' Blood said, ignoring the proffered handshake.

'Eh?'

'He means you, my dear Edward,' Coldwell creaked.

'If this is some kind of joke,' a red-faced Somersby began to bluster, but Coldwell quelled him with a look.

'I said we were here to receive these gentlemen's *full* report, Edward. They telegraphed me a *preliminary* report two days ago.'

'Keeler told me everything,' Blood said. 'You're in this as deep as a hog in a mud-hole, Somersby.'

'I don't intend to stay here and listen to . . . ' Somersby made to walk out, but a gesture from Coldwell brought Lee Chi to stand in the doorway and block his escape.

'Perhaps, Mr Blood, you could tell us briefly what you know about my brother-in-law's involvement in this affair?' Coldwell asked.

Blood leant against the wall of the carriage, his spare frame resting against the map of Paradise Valley. 'You were responsible for getting the railroad built,' he said to Somersby. 'You awarded contracts to build lengths of track, approved the payments, oversaw their satisfactory completion.'

'That's no crime,' Somersby sneered.

'It is when you and Keeler owned the three different contracting firms who built the line as far as Eden, though,' Tom said. 'Keeler told me everything before he died.'

'Dead?' Somersby asked in genuine surprise.

'A snake bite,' Jack told him. 'We think the snake survived.'

'You floated these companies with Keeler, accepted the inflated prices, and creamed off as much as thirty thousand dollars a mile of track. Keeler faked reports to make the going seem tougher than it was,' Blood continued.

'If we were making so much, then how is it we were involved with a gang whose express aim was to *stop* the railroad being built?' Somersby asked.

'You weren't at first,' Tom answered. 'The gang didn't start until Emory Hathersage began to make waves up in Washington, and it looked as if your little gold-mine would be closed down, the railroad forced to stop at Eden. So you brought the gang in, tried to make it look like it was in the pay of Hathersage. At the same time you got Hawkshaw and his gang to hit the ranchers and farmers on occasions, tried to stir up a war between them and the railroad so that the government would send the army in and Hathersage, if not killed, would be discredited and the open range would all be awarded to the railroad to sell to settlers and there'd be even more pickings for you. You almost succeeded.'

'But then the surveyor, Boyd, came to Keeler with some astounding news, didn't he?' Coldwell asked Somersby. 'He affects not to know, Mr Blood. Please tell me in detail.'

'Your original route was planned using the old army survey of the valley and surrounding mountains,' Blood said, turning and tapping the maps behind him. 'It was a hurried survey made during the so-called pacification wars against the Apaches of this area, the same ones in which Billy Free's tribe was wiped out. The main surveyor was a guy called Pearce, who was frightened for his hide. He took his scouts' word for some of his maps and surveys. He would have done as well to listen to the Apaches, like Boyd did.'

'And what do you mean by that, pray?' Somersby asked, his face pale with fear.

'Boyd got to know Billy Free through meeting Dan Johnson. Free told him the legend of the Dos Hermanas. That means the two sisters, the two big rocks at the entrance to the valley. They're supposed to be heading to a dance up in the Steins, invited by the gaans, the spirits who live there, but they've been turned to stone by evil spirits. Legend says that the gaans dance up there every moon to break the sisters free, and one day they'll dance down into the valley, and the sisters will finally dance away.'

'Very pretty,' Somersby sneered, 'but what has a child's tale to do with this?'

'Well, Henry Boyd figured maybe there was something behind this old story, so he asked Billy where the gaans danced, and Billy took him up onto High Mesa. That's where the railroad's supposed to go after it gets to the head of the valley.'

'Tell Edward what Boyd found,' Coldwell instructed, a thin smile on his face.

'Miles of moving land. It's partly volcanic spoil, and in other places follows a fault-line which feathers out over the whole mesa. The gods dancing up there are the minor movements of that fault-line. Regular earthquakes. There's no way a railroad track can be built over land like that.'

'But you were stuck with rails and ties for almost three hundred miles of railroad you couldn't build, weren't you?' Coldwell asked. 'And so Keeler decided to kill Boyd to keep him quiet. You'd continue to build to the head of the valley, then the pair of you would take your millions and disappear, leaving me with a railroad that went nowhere.'

'Boyd came to Keeler in his carriage and told him what he had found. Ben Chaney was there too,' Blood continued. 'It was the day that you and Mr Coldwell had visited the rail-camp and Chaney had been sacked for causing trouble. Keeler took Boyd at gunpoint out of the carriage, meaning to make him disappear out in the wilds somewhere, where a gunshot would not be heard by the rest of the camp, but he managed to escape and was only wounded. Keeler realized that everyone who knew about the survey had to be killed, so he sent the two deputies, Green and Collins, after Johnson, and faked the story about the pay-roll being stolen to implicate Boyd and Free as well as Johnson. Chaney was killed at the cave because he was of no further use, and couldn't leave the valley knowing as much as he did.'

'You have no proof whatsoever that I was involved in this,' Somersby snapped out, 'apart, that is, from the word of Keeler, a proven killer and cheat who is now dead.'

'Oh, we have lots of proof, Edward,' Hasland Coldwell said in his dry, creaky voice. He indicated the pile of papers on his desk. 'Yesterday, when I learnt of all this from Mr Blood, I, in the company of Lee Chi, of course, looked up the San Francisco addresses of the three contracting companies you and Keeler owned. What a surprise! They all shared the same office, a firm called the Territorial Development Company, the rent paid, incidentally, by you. Very sloppy. I — we — visited that place. No-one had been near for a day or two, but I secured the services of a none-too-respectable locksmith and we opened a rather well-hidden and secure safe we found there. Inside were bank-books for you and Keeler, and a huge amount of stock in the Northern Railroad, my competitor, I am sorry to say, and a lot of money in bank-notes, plus documents and letters which would implicate you directly and which would put you in jail for a very long time.'

Somersby's mouth opened and closed. There was nothing he could say.

'It is rather ironic,' Coldwell said,

'but you have been doing my work for me for quite a while, Edward. You see, I had thought for a long time, since my sister took up with you, in fact, that you were a bad one. So, I kept you close and waited for you to go wrong. I missed the false contracting scheme at first. It's taken Mr Blood to spot it.' He broke off and turned to Tom and Jack. 'I really should have seen what he was up to,' he confided. 'The idea is not new. It was originally perpetrated in France, known as the Credit Mobilier, and has been successfully worked over here also by the directors of the Union Pacific.'

'Yeah. I heard of it,' Blood said.

'So,' Coldwell continued, staring coldly at Somersby, 'although I kept you close and gave you an important post in my business, for my sister's sake, I never trusted you, Edward, nor did I take you fully into my confidence. I decided several months ago that the railroad would end at Eden, as the northern route was far more preferable.

However, once it became known what I had decided, the stock on the northern route would go up, so I bought secretly, at a low price per bond, and allowed my railroad to carry on some small distance beyond Eden, so no-one should suspect what I was up to. Now, with the rest of this stock in the northern route, which you are about to sign over to me, I own a goodly percentage, a controlling share, I would say, even.'

'And if I don't sign it over, what then?' Somersby asked.

Coldwell opened a drawer and took out a black-handled revolver. 'Then you will die, Edward,' he said simply. 'You will either blow your own brains out at this desk after writing a suicide note, or . . . ' here he nodded towards Lee Chi, 'it will be made to look as if you have. Then my sister will inherit all your stock and I will still control it. Either way you do not get to keep a single red cent you have stolen from me. At least if you sign you will be allowed to walk out of here, instead of being carried out in a box.'

There was a long silence in the carriage while Somersby looked at the grim faces before him and considered whether to call Coldwell's bluff. Coldwell's expression, and Lee Chi's lack of one, convinced him it was no bluff. 'Damn you,' he said finally, in a shaky voice. 'Give me the papers. I'll sign.'

Coldwell passed him some deeds of transfer and a pen, said with a little, satisfied laugh, 'I am already a very rich man, Mr Blood. With what I now own I shall be *extremely* wealthy in a very short time.'

'Now what?' Somersby demanded, throwing down the pen.

'I am afraid that I have some very bad news for you,' Coldwell said, leaning back in his chair and lacing his skeletal fingers together. 'Since I received Mr Blood's telegraph about you and Keeler I have been in telegraphic communication with my sister. You remember my sister, do you not, Edward? The one you duped to get close to my fortune?' He broke off and addressed Jack Storney. 'My sister looks much like me, Mr Storney. She is plain and in her thirties. An English accent like yours and a handsome face went far with her. She is however, a vengeful woman. She keeps what is hers. All of we Coldwells do. We are noted for it, as we are also for our longevity.' He turned back to Somersby, smiling thinly. 'The bad news is that my sister wants you back. She will have a very slow revenge on you, Edward, if you do come home.'

'Sounds worse than anything Billy Free could have invented,' Jack said, enjoying the look of fear on Somersby's once-haughty face.

'Or you can walk out of here on the understanding that I never see you again,' Coldwell said.

'You mean he walks free?' Blood said. 'After all the killings he's been behind?'

Coldwell raised an emaciated hand,

smiling grimly like a death's-head. 'Oh, it's merely a matter of time with someone like Edward Somersby — I wonder if that's your real name, by the by, Edward? I also wonder just what your end will be? I don't think it will be long. A knife in the ribs in some crooked card-game? Madness and a slow death by syphilis, caught from some cheap doxy in the red light area of 'Frisco? Maybe the whiskey bottle will get you, or a living death from opium addiction in some waterfront den by the docks — oh, yes, I know about your little laudanum habit, Edward. You have almost every vice and no redeeming virtue, do you? It shouldn't take you long to dig your grave.'

'Save me the lecture, you old bag of bones,' Somersby growled. 'I'm walking out now, and I hope to God I never see you or your poxy sister again!'

As he approached the door Coldwell made a sign to Lee Chi, who gripped Somersby by the shoulder. 'Wallet,' Coldwell said, and Lee Chi frisked

Somersby and threw the wallet over to his master. Coldwell took all but a few dollars from the wallet, then threw it at Somersby's elegantly-shod feet.

'I have left you enough for a rail-ticket to San Francisco and the price of a cup of coffee when you get there,' he said. 'I should imagine that's more than you came to me with. You may now go to hell in your own way, but make no mistake, if at any time in your desperation you think to show your face at my door, or to presume on any of my friends, even to mention that you know me, I shall have you killed. That is all. Now you may go.'

Coldwell made a sign to Lee Chi; he let go his grip and Edward Somersby slunk out.

Coldwell gazed at the open door for a full minute, then wiped a hand down his face before turning to Tom and Jack. 'I must congratulate you both on a job well done. What made you first suspect him, Mr Blood?'

'I knew it was someone who was

close to the centre of things when the telegraphed newspaper article was sent to Eden, warning that we were coming,' Blood said, 'and for a time I even suspected you. The editor of the *Eden Times* told me that Jake Dawson was known to you, that you had sent him with a recommendation to the town of Eden after Bob Croft was killed. But when I mentioned to Dawson that I understood he was a personal friend of yours he looked mystified. So I figured it was someone who knew you well, could have forged a letter of recommendation, and OK'd it on personal visits even. Then widow Croft told me about a guy who came to her farm with Keeler when the railroad was first planned, tried to buy her husband, get him to do the kind of work for Keeler and Somersby that Dawson was prepared to do.'

'I remember her telling you about that,' Jack said. 'She said the stranger was tall and slim, good-looking. Was that what made you suspect Somersby?'

'Partly,' said Blood. 'What clinched it was she said he held his mouth in a strange way. Remember that the widow was nearly stone deaf, and read lips. The man *would* hold his mouth differently if he spoke with an upper class English accent. You speak the same as Somersby, Jack.'

'Yes, well there the similarity ends,' Jack said with a sniff.

'But neither of you move your top lip,' said Blood with a smile. 'You hold your mouth strangely when you speak, just as Amy Croft said that man did. That's what told me it was Somersby behind all this.'

* * *

'So, where to now, Tom?' Jack asked as they stepped down from the president's carriage.

' 'Frisco, for a bath and a few days' rest,' Tom said, leaning against the carriage to put a smoke together. 'Then I think I'll take a trip up to Missoula on the *Old Independent*, see if Chad Layne is still short of deputies. I reckon someone ought to be with him when he goes to visit that Gaits, the rancher who was sheltering the gang we put away, at the start of this whole damned mess. You coming with me?'

Jack shook his head. 'No, Tom. I've been doing some thinking, and I do believe you're right. I'm not cut out for this game. I'm going back to the valley, going courting, marry the woman if she'll have me.'

Tom laughed softly. 'I knew it! That Laura Hathersage got under your skin, huh?'

Jack's eyes widened in surprise. 'Good God, no, old chap!' he drawled. 'Didn't you see her when Keeler was trussed up and being squeezed to death? She practically swooned with pleasure. She's dashed handy with that whip, too. Last lady I met with her predilections was in a bordello in New Orleans! Feller who marries her is going to have an even more demanding job than the one

I've been doing of late!'

'So who's the lucky lady, Jack?'

'Amy Croft,' Jack said. 'What a woman. Brave, loyal, beautiful. My heart went out to her that day when we first met her and she spoke of how she'd lost the two men she'd loved. Dan Johnson was a fool. He should have stuck with Amy. So, I'm going back to her farm, and if she'll take me as her husband I'll be the happiest man in Paradise!'

Neither of them had heard the massive Lee Chi as he descended the steps in his soft Chinese slippers. Now he stood before them, hands in his sleeves, and bowed.

'Your friend who was killed,' he said. 'He die bravely? I think he true fighter, like us?'

'Yeah, he took two with him,' said Blood.

'Ah,' said Lee Chi. 'Good. I am Buddhist. Tonight I burn joss-sticks, say prayer. Your friend reborn in good place.'

'Thanks,' said Tom. 'He'd like that.'

'When he speak to me, he call me dwarf,' said the giant Lee Chi. 'That very funny, I think, when he say. Also, he tell me to go whistle *Dixie*.'

'That's right,' said Jack with a laugh, 'so he did!'

'I learn, to surprise him when he come back,' said Lee Chi, with a broad smile, and pursing up his lips he began to whistle 'Away Down South in Dixie', though some of the notes wandered a mite.

THE END

We do hope that you have enjoyed reading this large print book.

Did you know that all of our titles are available for purchase?

We publish a wide range of high quality large print books including:

Romances, Mysteries, Classics
General Fiction
Non Fiction and Westerns

Special interest titles available in large print are:

The Little Oxford Dictionary
Music Book, Song Book
Hymn Book, Service Book

Also available from us courtesy of Oxford University Press:

Young Readers' Dictionary
(large print edition)
Young Readers' Thesaurus
(large print edition)

For further information or a free brochure, please contact us at:

Ulverscroft Large Print Books Ltd.,
The Green, Bradgate Road, Anstey,
Leicester, LE7 7FU, England.
Tel: (00 44) **0116 236 4325**
Fax: (00 44) **0116 234 0205**